Merrily
MATCHED

CATHRYN BROWN

DEAR READER

Merrily Matched picks up the story of Molly, Aimee's friend in *Hopefully Matched.* She's the owner of Cinnamon Bakery, and someone who owns a bakery filled with sweet holiday treats deserves to find romance at Christmas.

Even if she isn't looking for it.

This book is back in Homer, Alaska, one of my favorite places on Earth. It's a charming small town that my family made many happy memories in. The natural beauty there is untouched. Tall mountains—snow-covered in this story —meet a beautiful bay.

Joe's the new veterinarian in town. Molly's holiday season is turned upside down when she meets Noelle, an Alaskan malamute dog. Who could be more perfect as a couple than a handsome veterinarian and a brand new dog owner?

I hope you enjoy their story!

CHAPTER ONE

*C*hristmas music blasted through the room.

"Aimee, I know you love that song, but please turn it down!" Molly shouted over the din. Seconds later, the quiet melody of the song filled Cinnamon Bakery.

Even so, the sound of it ramped up Molly's stress another notch.

Her friend brought over a stack of napkins and began refilling the dispenser near the cash register. "This year, you're a Scrooge."

"You don't need to help me here. You have your own business to run." Molly straightened a tray of decorated sugar cookies and slid them into the glass display case. Had her change of subject distracted her friend?

Aimee shrugged. "Now that I'm moving out of my store, I have more time to do things I enjoy."

"And you enjoy helping here?"

Aimee stared at her. "Don't think I didn't notice that you changed the subject, Molly Becker. You used to love Christmas music."

Molly turned away and went to get more cookies so Aimee couldn't see her expression. To say this song and every Christmas song stressed her out was an understatement. *Everything* about Christmas stressed her out. "I always enjoyed this song," she whispered. "What happened?"

"I heard what you said." Her friend crossed her arms. "You said *enjoyed,* not enjoy. Past tense."

Molly returned with a tray of cinnamon sugar cookies. With it safely on the display shelf in the case, she swallowed hard and turned to her friend, not ready for the coming discussion. "You're right."

"I'm right? That's your answer? I know I'm right. My question is: *why* are you acting this way?"

Molly straightened. "Do you remember Silas?"

Aimee shrugged. "Sure, he's the man you dated . . . last Christmas. Is that it? A Christmas breakup?"

"Sort of. Every time I saw him or talked to him, he complained about my business intruding on 'us' time. By the time it was Christmas Eve—"

"You'd had enough. You broke up with him that day, didn't you?"

Molly sighed. "I did, but I should have done it earlier. I refuse to go through that again. Even Christmas music reminds me of it. The good news is that if I focus on my bakery, I should have enough for a down payment on a house by January."

"Congratulations! Jack and I hope to buy a house next year too."

"As to having time for romance, look around you." She gestured at the row of glass cases. "My display cases are loaded with sweets that I've been baking since early this morning. As soon as I open the doors, the shelves will start emptying out, and I'll have to make more."

Aimee put her hands on her hips and raised an eyebrow. "You're telling me what happens every day, Scrooge."

"But it's almost time for the tree lighting and other holiday activities that bring visitors to our small town. Those put everyone in even more of a holiday food mood. And I ship baked goods on top of that. I'm too busy for romance."

At least that was what Silas had told her.

Aimee frowned. "Having steady business is good. I don't understand."

"Steady, yes. Barely being able to keep up . . . not as much fun."

"That I *do* understand. It's why I closed my storefront. But you're the one who decided to ship treats around the state. You could stop that."

"Joy to the World" started playing and brought her into the moment. A smile began, and scents of gingerbread mingled with cinnamon rolls wafted past her nose. *Maybe she could relax a bit.* Then the kitchen timer sounded because she needed to check on both of those treats. On the way, she realized that if she didn't start another batch of each, she'd fall behind.

Molly spoke loudly from her baking area. "Nope. It all goes to my down payment. Besides, I've set up my life so I can manage all of this. I even cooked and froze meals. I can go home and heat them up. Everything I earn will go into savings." And then she wouldn't have time to think about dating and mistletoe and all things romance.

Aimee raised an eyebrow. "I hope your life will go smoothly over the next month."

"You can count on it." Molly gave a single nod. She wouldn't allow anything to mess up her plans. "Now, I need to get to work making the next batch. And I still have to pack up the cookies to ship."

Aimee frowned.

"What?"

"I'm worried about you being so busy that you can't even enjoy the holidays. Or anything, for that matter. Maybe hire some help. I know you've done that every once in a while. I'm sure some college students will be home on break soon."

"I'm considering that." And she was. She did want to see, though, if she could do it herself, along with her mom's part-time help waiting tables, and save that amount toward her house. "But I always have my business-first policy. Putting it first has gotten me through a couple years of owning Cinnamon. This Christmas could push me over."

"Push you over into exhaustion, and maybe even a life you don't want to live."

"It's a happy life."

"What about a kiss under the mistletoe? Wouldn't you like to have someone special to spend the holidays with?"

Laughter bubbled up inside Molly at Aimee's dreamy expression. "Spoken like someone in love." Though it was still early in the morning, a couple walked by her bakery. Holding hands, they also looked happy. "No, I've had my heart broken too many times. I went on so many first and second and third dates. There have been a couple that lasted somewhat longer than that—like Silas. Every single time, my heart was broken."

Sympathy shone in her friend's eyes. "I never realized that was how you felt. Sure, I knew that you always pointed out the handsome man in the room, and you often got the date with him. I didn't realize you'd been hurt because you always bounced back."

Molly waved the thought away. "I'm fine. I learned my lesson from watching you and Jack. You didn't have to chase him. My chasing days are over."

Aimee checked her watch. "Sorry to cut this short, but I have to get to my jewelry store." Aimee walked toward the door.

Molly put a muffin in a bag and followed her over. She unlocked the door so her friend could leave.

But Aimee hadn't finished. "People meet the loves of

their lives in a lot of different ways, and sometimes it's the way you did it in the past. Maybe the next customer to come through there"—Aimee tapped on the bakery's door —"is the right one for you."

Molly could see movement outside and recognized a favorite customer. "I predict that the next person to come to the door is female and old enough to be my grandparent." They stepped aside as the door pushed open, and a woman with fashionably styled gray hair entered. Cinnamon wasn't officially open, but Molly would serve her anyway.

Molly said, "Choose any table you'd like, Mrs. Jacobsen. I'll be right over." She turned toward her friend. "I'm fine. I just hope that someday I meet someone who makes me get the same goofy grin on my face that you do every time I mention the word 'Jack.'"

Aimee put her hands on her cheeks and turned a vivid shade of red. "I didn't realize I did that, but as soon as you said his name I could feel what happened to my face. That is so embarrassing!"

Molly handed the bag to Aimee. "I'd be worried about you if you didn't get that look. Do me a favor and taste this muffin. It's a new one I'm trying for the holidays, a spin on my cranberry-orange muffin because the muffin itself is chocolate. Tell me what you think."

Aimee took the bag. "I will be happy to be your taste tester once again. I only have a few more months in my Homer Gems storefront. Then I'll be working from my home studio, and I can stop by more often."

At Molly's unintended pained expression, she added, "And I promise not to push you into dating. Much."

Laughing, Molly said, "I'm always happy to have you here. I may be interested in dating. Definitely not this Christmas, though." A second later, Molly asked, "You gave notice for the end of the year? I hadn't realized it was a firm date."

"I told my landlord that I was ready to move out any time. I seriously doubt he will find anyone to take that space before the first of the year, so I'll be there through Christmas. Maybe I'll bring in some extra money for the wedding."

Molly hurried over to her customer's table as soon as Aimee left. "Mrs. Jacobsen, it's always great to see you." As soon as the words were out of her mouth, Molly realized that something was wrong with her frequent patron. The elderly woman had an air of defeat Molly had never seen before.

"This is my last time coming here for a while. Maybe forever."

Molly pulled out a chair at the table and sat next to the elderly woman. "Oh, no! Are you having health problems?" As soon as she spoke, she realized she'd crossed a line. "Never mind. It's none of my business."

Mrs. Jacobsen patted Molly's hand. "No, dear. You've always been kind, so I don't mind the question. I'm happy to share that I'm perfectly healthy. My problem is that I turned eighty, and my daughter and grandchildren decided they would like to have me nearer to them in Anchorage."

Molly leaned back in her chair. This woman might be of a certain age, but nothing about her said *feeble*. Right now, she wore jeans, a rhinestone-studded T-shirt, and a jean jacket, and had a faux fur coat laying over the back of the chair. She'd complained a couple of years ago when she'd had to stop wearing high heels and go for more comfortable shoes. Even then, they'd been stylish.

She always had a spring in her step, and Molly knew she could often be seen walking Homer's beaches for exercise. When Molly didn't say anything, the woman continued.

"I must admit that I don't enjoy the four-and-a-half hour drive to Anchorage as much as I did in the past. Now that I'm getting great-grandchildren, it would be nice to see them more often." The older woman wiped a tear from her eye.

"I'm sure it'll be fine." Molly wasn't, but what else could she say?

"Oh, I'll adapt. I'll adjust. My daughter even remodeled a section of her house so I can have my own private space. It even has a kitchen."

"That's wonderful!"

"She's a lovely woman." Then Mrs. Jacobsen frowned. "I'm not sure how I bore a child like this, but she does not like dogs." The woman raised sad eyes toward Molly. "I have to give up my Noelle."

"Have you had her long?"

"She's five years old. I got her when she was an adorable puppy. I'm going to drop her off at the shelter because no one I know is able to take another pet." She wiped her eyes again. "People always seem to want puppies, so the fate of a little older dog in a shelter may not be good." Now, tears streamed down the woman's face.

Molly raced over and grabbed a box of tissues from behind the counter.

"Thank you, my dear." Mrs. Jacobsen took one and dabbed her cheeks with it. "This isn't your problem. I stopped here to get a dozen of your cinnamon rolls to take with me. I want to share a bit of Homer with my family when I arrive."

Molly rubbed the woman's shoulder as she stood, then packaged up her treats. She thought about the dog as she brought the box over. Growing up, she'd wanted a dog. Any dog. Her mom was very much like Mrs. Jacobsen's daughter. She was a lovely woman, kind and friendly, but she'd never allowed them to have any pets. No matter how many times Molly had begged for a dog when she was growing up, her mother had always said, "We just don't have time," or some other excuse.

"I've always wanted a dog." Molly heard a wistful note in her voice.

Mrs. Jacobsen jumped to her feet. "Thank you! Thank you!"

Molly watched her leave, wondering what on earth she'd done that was so amazing. Then she realized the other woman had forgotten her cinnamon rolls. As Molly picked them up and took a step toward the door, Mrs. Jacobsen returned with a big leashed dog, a bulging plastic trash bag, and what appeared to be a dog bed.

"You've always been so kind to me when I've been in here. I know you'll take great care of Noelle." She set the bag on the floor and handed Molly the end of the leash. Rubbing the dog's head, she said, "You be a good girl for Molly." Then she pulled out a key ring and put it on the table. "This is to my house on East End Road."

When she rattled off an address, Molly pulled out her phone and entered it there.

"I told my family I would move, but I'm not selling, so I can still spend time here in my own place. You're welcome to go out there. It might even help Noelle with the transition if she's in her familiar place. She's an Alaskan malamute, and they like to run." The older woman took the cinnamon rolls from Molly's hands. "What do I owe you for these?"

Molly shook her head. "They're my going-away present for you."

The woman brightened at that. Then she reached down and gently rubbed the dog behind her ears. "Malamutes are furry dogs, so please remember to brush her every few days."

She waved and hurried out to her car, leaving Molly completely shell-shocked.

Molly held the leash of the large Alaskan malamute that she now seemed to own. "Noelle, what just happened?"

She had a dog. She had *no* idea how to take care of a dog.

CHAPTER TWO

When Joe opened the door to Cinnamon Bakery, the scent of cinnamon and other spices floated out to him. The sign said they weren't open, but he'd watched an older woman leave as he'd walked up the sidewalk. Taking a deep breath, he stepped inside, and his eyes immediately went to an attractive blonde in a pink apron standing in the middle of the room.

She shook her head as though to clear it. "What just happened?"

"Excuse me?"

Appearing to notice him for the first time, she turned a bright shade of red and said, "I was talking to myself. Can I help you? Wait, I can't." An exasperated expression on her face, she looked down at one of the prettiest dogs he'd seen in a while.

Joe slowly crossed over to the dog and knelt. "Do you mind if I pet your dog?"

"Not at all. But I should warn you that I don't know if she bites or not."

He held out his hand, and the dog lapped her tongue across it. Ruffling her ears, he laughed. "This one is sweet. Malamutes usually love people. Not that he or she wouldn't be assertive if it felt threatened."

"Good to know."

"What's your name, pretty girl?"

"Molly."

He scratched behind the dog's ears. "You're a good dog, Molly, aren't you?"

The woman groaned. "Sorry. She's Noelle. I'm Molly. My brain seems to have left along with Mrs. Jacobsen."

Joe chuckled. "It sounds like there's a story there." It surprised him that he wanted to hear it. He wasn't one for chitchat. He usually wanted the facts and then moved on —probably due to years of fast-paced medical schooling. He had time now, though.

A chirping noise came from the back of her bakery.

"I need to pull cookies out of the oven before they burn." She held the leash up. "But I can't."

"I'll take care of her. I would never want to stand in the way of a cookie."

Molly thrust the leash in his hands and hurried off with the words, "Thank you!"

While she was gone, he glanced around the café. It had a slightly old-fashioned look with small white tables and pink decorations. It could have seemed too feminine if the scent of baked treats hadn't overrun everything else in his mind.

Molly returned a few minutes later with a cookie on a plate. Chocolate chip, if he wasn't mistaken. "It's still warm, so be careful." She pulled it back. "Unless you don't like chocolate."

"I love anything that smells that good."

When she grinned as she handed the cookie to him, his heart beat double-time. As he ate, he realized that there should have been other people in the restaurant. "Why am I your only customer?"

She shrugged. "I'm technically not open for another few minutes. When I saw one of my favorite customers coming this way, I opened early for her."

"Would that be Mrs. Jacobsen?"

"Yes. Noelle is her dog. *Was* her dog." She stared at Noelle with a mixture of fear and wonder.

"She's yours now?"

Molly softly said, "She is." She reached down and tentatively petted the dog's head.

"I'm new to Alaska, but I'd be surprised if dogs were allowed in restaurants. Not that I wouldn't vote to let them in, but . . ."

Molly's mouth opened in an O. "What am I going to do with her?"

Noelle took that moment to talk in the typical malamute way—a mixture of chattering and whimpering. Molly put her hand over her heart and took a step back. "Are you sure she isn't a mean dog?"

He did his best not to laugh. "She's just talking to you. Most malamutes don't bark unless there's danger. They make sounds like what you just heard."

She cocked her head to the side. "I'm glad you stopped by when you did. I'm Molly Becker, the owner of this bakery."

"Joseph Wiseman. Joe." He wouldn't have any problem remembering her name, which was a good thing since he'd have a lot of names to remember as he met his neighbors.

"It's nice to meet you, Joe." She checked her watch. "I need to open." Her eyes went to the dog. "But you're right that a dog in here would break state health codes."

"I could keep her for the day."

Her expression said she didn't trust him. "I'm sorry, but I can't turn her over to someone I just met. What would I say to Mrs. Jacobsen if I lost her?" She put her hand over her mouth. "Not that you would take her. Wait! I know! Could you watch the bakery for a few minutes?"

He took a step backward. Why would she trust a stranger? Then he realized that if he wanted to make friends in Homer, this would be a good place to start. "I don't know how to run a bakery. Why is that better than watching the dog?"

"At this moment, I'm more willing to risk that. Besides, it's easy. Wash your hands, put on some gloves, and write down what everybody bought along with their name and phone number. If they want to eat here, put it on a plate. If they're taking it out, put it in a box."

Molly grabbed the leash and hurried to the door with Noelle at her side. "Fortunately, this time of year almost everyone who comes in is a resident, and I'll be able to tag them the next time they stop by." She opened the door. "That makes me ask: do you live around here?"

"Yes, I do." He didn't add, *as of yesterday.* That might have removed some of her oddly placed trust in him.

She gave a nod, closed the door, and was gone.

Just two days in his new hometown and he was starting to wonder what he'd gotten himself into. But he'd never lived in a small town before, so maybe this was how things worked.

Joe stared at the closed door. What had happened? The sign above the shop—*Cinnamon Bakery*—had caught his attention. What man doesn't love a cinnamon roll? He'd stepped inside, seen a pretty girl, and then noticed her dog. A dog in a restaurant.

Now he was in charge of a bakery.

The door opened, and an older man wearing a winter coat over a flannel shirt and jeans entered. He stopped, looked around, and turned toward Joe.

Putting on his new baker's assistant role, Joe smiled and said, "Can I help you?"

"Where's Molly?"

"She had to step away, and she asked me to fill in for her."

The man eyed him with more than a small amount of suspicion before stepping forward. "I don't believe we've met."

"I'm Joe Wiseman. I'm a veterinarian who will be opening a new clinic soon."

At that, the man seemed to relax a little. He ordered his cinnamon roll to eat there along with a cup of coffee. Joe wondered if it was so he could keep an eye on the place. He assumed that would be one of the perks of living in a small town. While some might find that stifling, he thought he would enjoy that sense of security, something he hadn't experienced when living alone in a big city.

CHAPTER THREE

$\mathcal{M}$olly hurried down the sidewalk with Mrs. Jacobsen's dog's leash—correction: *her* dog's leash—in her hand. Noelle's fluffy tail was down, not happily wagging. Maybe she knew her owner had left her. Molly hoped Aimee could watch Noelle this morning. Her friend had to know more about dogs than she did.

When she'd been a child, Molly had pictured her dream dog as a dachshund or maybe a cocker spaniel. Noelle had to be at least twice that size. No matter what, though, she now owned a malamute.

She raced into Homer Gems. "Aimee!"

The sound of tools dropping was followed by rushing footsteps as her friend hurried around the corner. "What's wrong?"

"I just got a dog."

Aimee's gaze dropped to the large white-and-gray dog

at Molly's side. "That's a surprise. Do you know *anything* about dogs?"

"I know that I now own one. Can you watch her until Mom arrives for her shift? I'll run her over to my apartment then."

Aimee kept her eye on the dog as she stepped closer. "It's pretty quiet in here right now. I guess I can tie her up in the back if a customer comes in. What's her name?"

Molly looked down at the dog at her side. "Noelle." She passed the leash to her friend.

"I'm sure there's a story to this. Does she have food and water bowls?"

Molly rolled her eyes. "She needs those, doesn't she? Mrs. Jacobsen brought in a big bag along with the dog, so they're probably in there."

Aimee shook her head as though to clear it. "Mrs. Jacobsen?" She held up one hand to stop Molly from speaking. "Never mind. You need to get back to the bakery. You can tell me all about this later. I'm sure that Noelle and I will have a good morning together." She reached down and petted the head of the large dog. "Aren't we going to have a good time?" When the dog licked her outstretched hand, Aimee giggled.

Seeing that her new companion was well taken care of, Molly ran back out the door and up the street. As she did, she realized that she'd left her bakery with a complete stranger. A handsome one with brown hair and blue eyes, but still someone she didn't know. She hoped everything would be okay when she returned.

Ten minutes after Joe had been left in charge, he had a tally of a dozen names and what they had ordered. He didn't even know how much each thing cost, so he couldn't help out there. The one woman who had wanted a fancy coffee drink had left instead with black coffee with cream and sugar. How was he supposed to know how to run those complicated machines without lessons?

By that ten-minute mark, Joe felt as overwhelmed as he had on his first day of veterinary clinical trials. No, more so. At least then he'd had enough training to know how to do the basics and take care of the animals. Here, he didn't have a clue.

When Molly hurried through the door, Joe had never been happier to see anyone in his life. When his first customer saw her, he got up and left, apparently having confirmed that Joe was indeed taking care of her place.

She hurried behind the counter, washed her hands, and pulled on a pink apron. At least she hadn't expected him to wear one.

"Thank you! I got Noelle over to my friend." She chewed on her lip. "I just hope she's okay being there."

He was as confused as he had been during his specialty coffee attempt. "Why isn't she at your home instead of here?"

"As I explained to you, I got Noelle two minutes before you walked in." At his puzzled look, she continued. "My customer arrived here upset that she was going to have to give up her dog because she was moving in with her daughter and grandchildren in Anchorage."

She bustled around, checking out everything in the back, as she continued. "One minute I was saying I always wanted a dog—because I always did, but my mother never wanted one—and the next minute I was standing there with my own dog. Mrs. Jacobsen is a petite older lady. I expected her dog to be like one of those small dogs ladies put in their purse and carry around. Something that would be really easy to have in my apartment. But no."

He chuckled. "Instead, you have an Alaskan malamute. Not the smallest breed of dog on the planet."

"That's certainly true." She hurried out to check with each of her customers and came back to make fancy coffees for a couple of them. When that was done, she returned to where he still stood at the cash register. "Joe, I've taken a lot of your morning, and I'm sure I've provided some entertainment you had not anticipated. Can I get you anything to eat on the house?"

"I enjoyed the cookie. But what's the best thing you've got?"

A smile lit up her face, and her eyes sparkled. "I sell more cinnamon rolls than anything else." She leaned closer to him and lowered her voice. "But my personal favorite is the brownie with a white chocolate swirl that I make only during the holidays."

His mouth watered. A few minutes later, he left the bakery with his bag of treats that included a brownie *and* a cinnamon roll.

So far, everyone he'd met in this town had been friendly. Since Homer was his new home, that was a very good thing.

A short distance down the street, he stopped in front of a jewelry store that had a *For Lease* sign in the window.

He turned to check out the area filled with shops which would mean good visibility for his new veterinary clinic. Being on a city street, though, instead of in a separate building meant that parking would be a problem. He needed his clients to be able to load and unload their pets.

A half-filled parking lot not far away caught his attention. He snapped a photo of the lease sign before going toward the parking lot to check it out.

As he got closer, he could tell that this could work. Since they weren't using all the spaces, he might be able to negotiate with them to permanently use some of them for his veterinary practice.

He opened the bag and chose the brownie. Taking a bite, he turned back to the jewelry store and pictured his clients bringing in their pets from this lot. Maybe Homer would be the place where he could finally put down roots and feel at home.

CHAPTER FOUR

*M*olly walked her dog to her car, wondering if it was okay to put a dog in a van she used for baked goods. But what choice did she really have? This was her only vehicle. Besides, there was a divider between the front seats and the back.

"Well, Noelle, we're going to see your new home," she said, opening the passenger door. "I hope you won't be too upset and miss your mom." The dog whimpered as though she understood. "I know. But you and I can be good buddies, can't we?"

The dog jumped into the van and up on the seat like a pro. She calmly sat there as they went down the road, but chattered when they passed vehicles with other dogs.

As she and Noelle walked up the steps to her second-floor apartment, Molly had a moment of panic. To save money, she'd recently moved into one of the least expensive places she could find. That meant "small" was an understatement.

She opened the door, and they went inside, with Noelle sniffing everywhere she could reach while leashed. When Molly closed the door and freed her, she zoomed around the apartment, zipping in and out of the bedroom, the bathroom, and the small kitchen area before coming back to look up at her with an expression that Molly could only read as, "Is this all there is?"

"I'm sorry, but this is it. I wasn't expecting to get you today. Or maybe ever. But we're going to make this work, aren't we?" She hesitated before she went back toward the door. "I'm going to leave you for a moment while I get all your things out of the car, including your dog bed. I'm sure you're going to be very happy when you have those."

Noelle chattered. This dog had the uncanny ability of making a response at the exact right moment. Molly wondered if she really did understand.

The evening passed rather uneventfully, with Noelle curled up on her dog bed and Molly searching every site online she could find for new dog owners, specifically those about Alaskan malamute dogs. This breed would "blow their coats" twice a year, a time when they shed massively. Molly winced when she envisioned the two of them trapped in a fur-filled apartment.

The next day, Molly came home in the middle of the day to take Noelle for a potty break. Her mother usually worked part-time in the bakery, but she'd asked her to work more hours for the holiday season. Having her there every day had turned out to be more important than she'd expected.

After what seemed like a long afternoon at the bakery, she stopped at the grocery store. When she'd poured all but a small amount of the food Mrs. Jacobsen had given her into Noelle's bowl that morning, she'd realized she had to add that to her shopping list.

After reading the ingredient list on several bags, Molly chose a dog food that appeared to be healthy and would probably be less expensive than the one Noelle's former owner had used.

As she dropped her heavy winter coat on the sofa, she noticed a sock she had left in the laundry basket now lying in the middle of the living room, slightly chewed. Holding it up, she asked her canine companion, "Did you get bored, Noelle?"

The dog, either to avoid confrontation or because she didn't want to admit her sins, didn't even glance her owner's direction. Either way, Molly chose to move the laundry basket to the shelf of her bedroom closet.

All in all, they seemed to be getting along well.

Molly poured the new food in the bowl and set it out for Noelle along with some water.

The dog came over, sniffed the food, sat down, and stared at it.

"I'm sure you'll love it. I know it's a different kind, but the bag said it was good for you."

Noelle sniffed the food again and must have decided it was okay because she started eating.

At least one thing was accomplished. When it came to humans, Molly definitely knew how to give them food they would love. Canines were all new.

When the dog dove into her food the next morning, Molly felt like she'd won the lottery.

Until she needed her shoes.

It seemed her new friend had become bored in the night. Molly went to work without matching shoes, but thankfully both were the same style, just one brown and one navy blue. Noelle had eaten some of Molly's most comfortable shoes, the ones she wore every day to work and that could stand up to long hours on her feet. They were also her most expensive. The one saving grace in all this was that Noelle had chewed one left and one right.

It might be December, but putting on boots only to take them off a few minutes later seemed pointless. There weren't any snow berms she needed to wade through when she went to or from her van, so she went inside Cinnamon already feeling foolish with her mismatched footwear.

She finished up her morning baking, once again wondering if she really needed to have an assistant. She'd been scrimping and saving for so long and was getting by as far as her time went, but this holiday season was going to test her.

She slid a tray of brownies into the oven. These had proven to be popular, so she mentally added them to the list of things to bake on the weekends when she knew the town would have a lot more visitors.

Molly walked in the door to her apartment and stopped. The arm of her sofa was . . . gone. Noelle lay curled up in her dog bed as though nothing had happened. It had been a secondhand couch she'd gotten for almost nothing, so the cost wasn't a factor. But the destruction was.

"Noelle, what have you done?"

She chattered a reply, which Molly took as a denial.

Molly sat on the remnants of her piece of furniture and stared at the ceiling. This month wasn't going anything like she'd expected. Definitely not to plan.

Turning toward her wayward charge, she said, "We're going to have to do something about this, aren't we? You aren't happy being locked up here all day. I can't say I blame you. You're a big dog, and this is a small place."

A knock on the door startled Molly. She jumped up and hurried over to look out the peephole. An angry man she recognized as the apartment manager stood there. She opened the door and stepped out, quickly closing it behind her. Was she allowed to have dogs? She really wasn't sure.

"What can I help you with today, Mr. Andino?"

"I've been getting complaints about a dog howling for hours."

He hadn't said from her apartment yet, so she kept smiling and waited for him to continue.

"You aren't allowed to have dogs here, Ms. Becker."

Her heart sank. "I'm not?" she said in a small voice.

"*Not.*" He crossed his arms and glared at her.

"I didn't get a dog on purpose."

Instead of asking how one accidentally owned a dog, he pursed his lips and frowned. Handing her a piece of paper, he said, "You have ten days to either move out or resolve this issue."

"Resolve how?"

"Get rid of the dog, of course."

He hurried away before she could say that she and this dog were stuck together.

CHAPTER FIVE

$\mathcal{M}$olly leaned against the door as she closed it. "We have a problem, Noelle."

This time, the dog was wise enough to remain silent.

Molly went into the tiny kitchen to get a glass of water. As she walked past the kitchen counter, the bone-shaped key ring with keys dangling from it caught her eye. She picked it up and looked over at her dog.

Maybe Noelle was unhappy because she'd not only lost her owner, who apparently had adored her, but she'd also lost her home, which included a place to run and play. At least Molly assumed there was a place to run and play. Almost anywhere in Homer would have more room than her chosen dwelling.

She tossed the keys in the air and caught them. "Noelle, we're going on a road trip." When she grabbed the leash, the dog started doing a dance around the room. Laughing, Molly said, "Hold still. We can't go unless I get this clipped on your collar." When she'd done that, she led —or, rather, Noelle led—them out to the van where the dog sat on the seat.

Molly closed the van's door and raced back into the apartment to grab enough food for dinner, hoping that Noelle could handle being alone in the van for three minutes without eating the passenger seat.

Once inside the van, she checked her phone for the address. She'd head through town for a distance and then down East End Road. She'd be surprised if this wasn't on at least an acre of land. As she was driving, she thought about Aimee and how Jack was out of town. She dialed her number, and as soon as her friend answered, said, "Would you like to come over for dinner?"

"Well, I certainly worked up an appetite with all my customers today."

"As in you really had a lot of customers or you're being sarcastic?"

"I actually had quite a few customers today. I sold several small things and got a new commission for a wedding ring set."

"Nice! I know you love doing those."

"Your call is perfect timing. Grandma and Grandpa went to Anchorage for a couple of days for some Christmas shopping, and I was going to be left to my own cooking."

Molly laughed. "I'm glad I saved you from that."

"Hey, I'm getting better at it."

Molly didn't want to touch that conversation, but she knew anything was a step up.

"I've been watching beginning cooking videos. Something about getting married makes me think I should know how to cook. Especially since Jack is every bit as bad in the kitchen as I am. I successfully made a grilled cheese sandwich this week."

Molly chuckled. "Well, if you'd rather fix another grilled cheese for tonight—"

"Don't you dare. I will be there. I'd better get back to work now. My jewelry-making ideas are flowing."

"Don't hang up! I'm not going to be at home. I'm going to be at Mrs. Jacobsen's, giving Noelle room to run."

"Okay. Text me the address, and I'll come over in a few hours."

Molly soon arrived at the driveway to Mrs. Jacobsen's home.

"You lived in a beautiful place, didn't you, Noelle?"

The dog perched on the seat next to her, and her tail started swishing as they drove closer to the house. A stone foundation topped by a cedar-planked house loomed in front of her. A wide porch wrapped around it. The steep roof with a wall of windows facing her told Molly that it must have a great room with a beautiful view. When she didn't see a fence, her shoulders tensed up with concern.

As soon as she opened the door, Noelle raced out of it and ran toward the house.

"Noelle, come here."

The dog stopped and looked at her as if asking, "Why? We're home, aren't we?"

When she's right, she's right. Molly followed behind and went up the steps to the front door. Mrs. Jacobsen may have known she was moving, but she apparently hadn't wanted to miss out on Christmas.

Garlands decorated every surface outside, and a Christmas tree stood on the deck. When Molly opened the door, she found a room with many decorations both large and small, but it somehow felt tasteful, not gaudy. Another Christmas tree had the place of honor in the middle of the room beside a stone fireplace that reached up to the peaked ceiling. This was exactly the kind of home Molly would have chosen. If only her budget allowed that.

She tossed her purse on a table and said, "Would you like to go outside and play? That's why we came here."

The dog beat her back to the door.

Molly found a stick in the snow and threw it for Noelle, who happily pranced back with it and dropped it at her feet. They played that game for about a half hour until the dog seemed to be slowing down.

Once both of them were inside again, Molly hung up her coat and rubbed her hands together to warm them. Wood stacked in the fireplace and long stick matches on the mantle told her this was a well-loved fireplace. She started a fire, and the room came to life.

"If you're okay here, I'm going to get our groceries out of the car."

Noelle flopped down by the fireplace, panting. *Mission accomplished.*

Molly brought in their things and started putting together the meal. When she heard a car's tires crunching on the snow, she went over to open the door.

Her friend stepped out of her car. "This is a beautiful house!"

"Tell me about it. I would love to live here."

Aimee entered and went straight over to the fireplace, stepping around the now-napping dog. "What did Mrs. Jacobsen say to you about the house?"

Molly thought back to the conversation. It had been just days ago, but seemed longer. Wasn't it a lifetime since she'd gotten Noelle? "She said something like I should come out here. That it was just going to be empty. And that Noelle would be happy here and loved running outside."

Aimee turned so the fire could warm her back. "Well, there you have your answer."

Molly felt like she'd missed the question. "What?"

"The answer to your problem. Noelle is happy here. Mrs. Jacobsen said you can stay here. End of conversation."

Molly waved her hands in front of her face. "Don't even think that. She said I could bring the dog over *to run.* Not that I should move in with everything I owned."

"In all fairness, I think what she said was somewhere in between."

Molly went over the conversation again in her mind. "I

wouldn't feel comfortable moving in unless I could pay Mrs. Jacobsen rent. Utilities are going to cost more if someone's living here."

"Well, it's something for you to think about, at least." Aimee sniffed the air. "What is that delicious scent?"

Molly laughed. "That, my friend, is chicken cordon bleu, scalloped potatoes, and broccoli."

"*I'll* move in if I can eat like that every dinner."

Molly might not have fashion sense that was worth anything or be able to keep a boyfriend, but she could cook like nobody's business. About twenty minutes later, they were seated at the dining room table in the corner of the great room. She suspected there would be a view—if it wasn't dinnertime in December and long after sunset.

Aimee spooned some of each item onto her plate, then hesitated for a moment. "There's something I need to tell you, and I don't want you to get upset about it because I've decided it's a good thing."

"It isn't about Jack, is it?"

"No, he's fine. We're fine. Of course, he keeps texting me ideas for weddings, which is very strange, considering his personality. Although, Jack does see things from an artistic viewpoint. I guess being a photographer and a former jeweler will do that to you."

Molly waited to eat in case this was terrible news. "Tell me, because I'm starting to imagine all sorts of bad things about your grandparents."

"No. *Everyone* is fine. It's just that someone has rented my store. The landlord called today to tell me."

"You mean they're going to move in after the holidays?" Molly took a bite of the chicken, and the cheesy goodness melted in her mouth exactly as it should. Then she noticed that Aimee had filled her plate but still not eaten anything.

"He would like to rent the building as soon as possible."

Without meaning to, Molly made a sound that came out as an angry growl.

Noelle lifted her head to see what had happened.

"I told you not to get upset. You know that I've wanted to get away from having a storefront. I'm very excited about only doing custom work and spending the day in my home studio."

Molly nodded. That was all her friend had been talking about for months. She took a bite of the scalloped potatoes and chewed slowly as she thought this over.

"What business is moving in?"

"We didn't talk about that." Aimee stared at her plate.

"Why aren't you eating? Doesn't it look good to you?"

"It looks delicious." Looking up at Molly, she blurted out, "The owner asked if I could be out by the end of the weekend, and I agreed."

Molly dropped her fork, and it hit the table with a clank. "You're being thrown out of your business? Today's Tuesday. That's less than a week! How are you going to do that?"

Aimee smiled. "I've had most of today to think about it, and I have figured almost everything out. When you close the bakery tomorrow, can you come over and help me with the boxes?"

Molly was about to say yes when she realized she now had a four-footed friend she needed to accommodate. When she glanced over at her, Aimee added, "Noelle will be fine. We can just keep her in the back of the jewelry store. She was good there the other day."

"Just make sure there's nothing she can chew on nearby." Molly laughed.

Grinning, Aimee put a bite of food in her mouth. "Oh, this is so good. Has she been eating you out of house and home?"

Molly grimaced and stared at the dog, who now calmly watched them eat. It was a testament to her dog's exhaustion that she hadn't come over to the table to ask for a taste from their plates. "She has actually *eaten* my house and home." Molly put her mismatched colored feet out where her friend could see them. "And you know that cheap but cute sofa that I used to have?"

Aimee gasped and put her hand over her mouth. "*Used* to have?"

"Well, I still have it, but it's not as cute now that one arm is missing."

"The whole arm? Wow." Aimee looked around. "Everything's in great shape here. Maybe she didn't like being cooped up in your apartment while you were gone."

"She did some of her chewing at night when I was there, asleep and unsuspecting."

"You may need to let her run a lot. Maybe at the beach or somewhere like that."

Molly sighed as she took another bite of her dinner. What options did she have? "You're probably right. My biggest problem is that we're being evicted."

Aimee gasped and reached for her water glass, coughing. After a swallow, she said, "No dogs allowed?"

Molly nodded. "I would normally suggest that I get up earlier so Noelle and I can go for a long walk, but my biggest problem is where I'm going to be living when I do that. The landlord gave me ten days' notice this afternoon."

"Call Mrs. Jacobsen and ask. No one is living in this house. It's probably better for her if someone is here and it isn't seen as an easy-to-break-into empty house."

Molly chewed on her lip. "It does sound good when you say that. I just don't know what she's going to think."

"From what you said, I think she'll do anything to keep her dog happy."

Molly picked up her phone and called Noelle's former owner. She explained the situation to her, and the older woman said, "I would love for you to live there! I thought of that when you agreed to take my precious Noelle, but I didn't want to intrude on your life any more than I already had."

A sense of wonder washed over Molly as she set down her phone after their conversation, which had included various things about the house.

"I can't tell from your expression if she liked or hated the idea."

Molly slowly said, "Mrs. Jacobsen told me she had wanted to suggest this all along. That I was welcome to stay here as long as I wanted to. Before I could even bring it up, she said she didn't even want any money for the utilities, that my taking care of Noelle was the nicest thing anybody had ever done for her. She was happy to help me out."

"You get to live here!"

Molly jumped to her feet, startling Noelle, who got on all fours and started howling.

"Noelle, we get to live here in your house."

The dog danced around, wagging her tail.

Aimee got up and hugged Molly. "This is so good. And you can put the money you aren't spending on rent toward buying your house."

Molly put her hands on her cheeks. "I hadn't thought of that. I can get a house for Noelle and me sooner than I'd hoped. This is what happens when you focus on your plan."

Aimee laughed so hard tears ran down her cheeks. "The plan disappeared when Noelle appeared. You have no plan."

Molly sheepishly grinned.

"We'd better eat this food before it gets cold."

Molly sat back down, and this time, Noelle trotted to her side. She stared at Molly with an adoring expression.

"I forgot to ask your mom if you usually eat table food. But a bite of chicken shouldn't hurt, right?"

She cut the piece and lifted it up, the dog's eyes intently watching her every move. When Molly tossed it in the air, Noelle caught it, and it was gone in an instant. Molly laughed.

"You seem to be getting into this dog-ownership thing." Aimee spooned more scalloped potatoes onto her plate. "So tell me again about this focus you had for December. Every detail mapped out, didn't you say?"

"My business is still on track. And now that I've gotten Noelle settled, I think my personal life is back on track too."

Aimee was silent for a moment, and Molly wondered what she was thinking.

"What about men? I should rephrase that: what about a man?"

"Absolutely not. As I said before, this holiday season is man-free."

Aimee ate in silence again.

Molly put more chicken on her plate. When her friend still hadn't spoken by the time she finished it, she said, "Okay, what are you thinking?"

"I've seen this handsome man around town. He looks just your type."

At that, Molly burst out laughing. "And what is *my* type?"

"Handsome. Flannel shirts and denim."

Aimee knew her well. She didn't dress up very often, so she did appreciate a man who could look good casual.

"No wedding ring."

Molly grinned. "That is an important criterion. What does he do?"

Aimee furrowed her brow. "I don't know. I've seen him at the grocery store and near your bakery, but I've never spoken to him."

The man who'd helped her at her bakery the other day while she took Noelle down to Aimee's store came to mind. Joe.

She considered mentioning him to her friend, then decided against it. Now that Aimee's relationship with Jack had been ignited by a matchmaker, she knew her friend was anxious to do the same for someone else. Molly didn't want that someone else to be her. She had to stay firm that she didn't want a relationship now, especially not at Christmas.

As she thought about her friend, Aimee's business came to mind. She had a fairly large space filled with glass cabinets, jewelry, and everything else it took to run a brick-and-mortar store.

"I just realized something. How are you planning to move everything out of your store?"

"I have it all taken care of—including the help you so graciously offered."

"Your move will be more challenging than mine. The couch needs to be hauled to the dump, and I'll give the bed away since I don't need one here. I have a feeling that whatever furniture is in this house is much nicer than anything I had in my apartment. I can probably fit the rest in one van load." She brushed her hands together. "Easy."

"If you do need help, please call."

When Aimee had left, Molly snapped the leash on Noelle's collar and took her outside. She was going to have to have another chat with Mrs. Jacobsen to see if she should let the dog run. She didn't want to test any limits after dark, though, when she would have a hard time finding her again. Spotting a mostly white dog in the snow wouldn't be easy to do in the first place.

Later, tucked into a comfortable bed with a fluffy comforter, Molly felt like she'd checked into a wonderful country inn or bed-and-breakfast. This holiday season was already going so much better than she ever could have imagined.

CHAPTER SIX

*J*oe stopped on the sidewalk to watch the woman from the bakery—Molly. She stepped out of the home of his future veterinary practice carrying a cardboard box.

She was beautiful in an understated way, wearing jeans with a cream turtleneck sweater and a pink, heavy winter coat. He wasn't sure if the color in her cheeks and on her lips was natural or if she had used a small amount of makeup. Not that he had anything against makeup. His sisters were masters of the art. He just preferred simplicity.

Striding forward, he spoke when he neared her. "Can I help with that?"

She stopped and stared at him. "I can do this, Joe." She continued on her way and hefted the box into the back of a truck parked in front of the store.

He smiled at her and then asked again. "I have some spare time. Are you sure I can't help?"

Molly shrugged. "It's the middle of a weekday. I don't want to keep you from your work."

"I'll be setting up my business soon." He turned toward the storefront and envisioned it with the Wise Pets sign he'd ordered hanging above the windows. "It will be a few weeks before I get everything in order, and I'm back to working full time—often more than full time. I can help now, though." As he said the last sentence, another woman came out carrying a box.

She looked from Molly to him and then got a big grin on her face. "Of course we would like some help from a big, handsome man like you."

When Molly groaned at her friend's words, Joe hid a grin with a cough and a hand over his mouth. Then he introduced himself to her friend.

She answered, "I'm Aimee Jones. I owned a jewelry store here." Her words had a bittersweet tone, and she followed them by gesturing to the space he'd just leased. "I have to get everything out of here ASAP, so I welcome your help."

This would *not* be a good time to mention that he'd be the next tenant. Joe went inside, picked up a stack of boxes, and carried them out to the truck. He went back inside just in time to hear a conversation between the two friends.

Molly grabbed a box. "What do you have in these, Aimee, barbells?"

"Everything it takes to run a business. Joe can take that one."

He went to the stack. "Sure, leave it, and I'll do it."

Molly chuckled as she pulled open the door with one hand and held the box against the other hip. "My comment had nothing to do with whether I could carry it. Considering the weight of some things I have to heft in a bakery, this is easy."

Aimee picked up a box, and he followed her out. At the truck, Molly asked, "Tell me why we're doing this instead of your strong fiancé."

"Jack is on a photography expedition of sorts. He went to the Southeast, down by Sitka, where the weather's not too cold this time of year. We can do it ourselves with girl power."

Joe cleared his throat.

"I meant girls and you, of course, Joe."

He grinned. As they went inside, he realized that the room still held all of her jewelry display cases. He couldn't do anything until they were moved out. "What are you going to do with all of your glass cases?"

"I'm going to have to find a buyer for them. Right now, they're all going to be moved into storage. I have movers scheduled for tomorrow."

Molly jumped in. "Movers? I know Jack is out of town, but what about his brothers?"

"I didn't ask. They all have busy lives, and I didn't want to bother them."

Molly raised an eyebrow. "They seem to like helping

each other. How do you think it's going to go over when they find out you didn't call them when you needed help?"

Her friend was silent for a few seconds. "Probably not well. Maybe a couple of them could come on Saturday, and I can cancel the movers."

"Good plan."

"I'm happy to help, too, if you need it." He gave his number to Aimee. When the two women went outside to check something in the truck, he stayed behind, imagining his new clinic. He'd been the fourth vet in an office in Phoenix. Now, he would have a place of his own.

His family was as excited as he was about his new clinic. He could see them admiring it when they visited, and his dad—who could seem intense if you didn't know him—would beam with pride at his son's achievement. When Joe had chosen to help animals instead of people, he'd expected his physician father to be upset, but he'd supported him all the way.

He snapped a few photos to remind him what it looked like later when he sat down to plan the layout. Then he went back to helping Molly by carrying boxes.

CHAPTER SEVEN

*W*hile Molly added the ingredients to her commercial-sized mixer for sugar cookies, she thought about the time she'd spent with Joe moving the boxes out of Aimee's store, and a slow smile spread over her face. They'd stopped to chat between loads, and Aimee had been notably absent during those chats.

Molly liked being with him. But she would never chase a man again, and her track record said that she was not a good judge of character when it came to the male of the species. She and Noelle were doing just fine.

With five batches of cookie dough prepared, including white chocolate chip, gingerbread, and shortbread, Molly put everything in order for the morning and went home.

She knew something wasn't right the second she opened her new home's door. Noelle wasn't waiting there, ready to shoot out of it and play in the snow. Curled up in her bed, the dog lifted her head with a woeful expression on her face. Gone was the energy and bounce she'd had before.

"Are you okay?"

Noelle didn't move.

Molly knelt beside her and petted her head. "Don't you want to go outside and use the potty? Leash? Walk?"

The dog sighed and buried her head further down into the comfort of her dog bed. Something was very wrong.

Molly continued petting her. "I've had you for less than a week. I don't know what to do. Are dogs just like this sometimes, and you're actually okay?"

Noelle whimpered.

"You poor thing."

Noelle suddenly jumped to her feet and hurried over to the door. Molly opened it, and the dog went outside to do her business in a way that Molly could tell was not normal. She trudged back up the steps slowly and returned to her bed.

Molly had a sick dog on her hands, and it was late on a Saturday. She couldn't call her parents, because neither of them had ever owned a dog. Aimee had only spent time with dogs when visiting her grandparents.

She didn't want to do it, but there was an excellent answer.

Aimee had told her about a new vet in town who sounded very competent. She'd texted Molly the phone number yesterday with the note, "Just in case." Maybe someone who didn't have their practice set up yet would be more willing to come out at this hour. At least she hoped so because she didn't know how she could get this dog out of here, down the steps, and into her van.

She called the number, and a voice that sounded familiar answered.

Molly asked, "Is this the new veterinarian?"

His voice became more formal when he said, "Yes, do you have an emergency?"

Of course he'd gone to that thought because of the time.

"I'm not sure. My dog doesn't want to move." She explained the bathroom problem.

"Give me your address. I'll come right out to check on her."

Molly hung up the phone with a sigh. Her dog whimpered. This didn't look good. How was she going to tell Mrs. Jacobsen? Noelle was such a sweet dog. She felt like they were finally starting to bond. And now that she was happy in her own home—the much larger home with a huge yard—she'd even left her new owner's shoes alone.

A half hour later, a pickup truck pulled into the driveway and came to a stop. When the man stepped out of it and started walking toward her, the pieces fell into place. The man who had helped her out in the bakery and carried boxes for them. Joe Wiseman was the new veterinarian.

If she didn't know better, she would think that Aimee had somehow worked this out and set her up with Noelle's problem. But she knew her friend would never in a million years hurt an animal.

He came up the stairs with the bag in his hand, but stopped when he saw her. "Molly? Noelle is the sick dog?"

Near tears, she just nodded.

He put his hand on her arm. "Let me check her out. Where—" He started over toward Noelle when he spotted her. As he examined her, he said, "Tell me about what you've been feeding her, if there's anything new in her diet recently."

"Remember I had just gotten her the morning you found her in my bakery?"

He glanced up at her for a moment. "I forgot about that. You seem like you've been together longer."

"Noelle and I met five minutes before you walked in the door. As to her diet, let me get out what I've been feeding her. It's not the same thing that Mrs. Jacobsen was giving her. I found this at the store, and it looked like it would be good."

He rocked back on his heels and looked up at her. "You completely changed the dog's diet?"

Molly turned around slowly with the bag of dog food in her hands. In a low voice, she asked, "Did I do a bad thing?"

"That's probably what's wrong. When you change an animal's diet, you need to do it slowly—mix the old food with the new. Sometimes it upsets their stomachs when you do it abruptly. I think that's what's happened. She doesn't have a temperature. I don't feel anything unusual when I examine physically. Her eyes look okay. In short, I don't *think* anything else is wrong with her."

"You don't think or you're sure?"

"Molly, it's just the same as it would be with a human. Part of what I do is a best guess. I look at the symptoms and all the known facts. Then I come up with an idea of what the least invasive fix would be for the problem. Right now, that would be putting her back on the food she was used to and mixing it with bland canned food to help get her back on her feet more quickly."

"I don't have any more of the old food. Where am I going to get that in Homer at this hour? The pet stores are all closed, and I think that food is too specialized for the grocery store."

"Good point." He ran his hands through his hair, leaving it standing up straight in places when he stopped. "I'm used to city life where you can get almost anything you want most of the time. For tonight, we can try a bland diet of chicken and rice."

"I can do that. There's actually food in a big freezer in the garage. I'll get some chicken out. The owner probably has rice in the cupboards."

He picked up his bag and stood. "The owner?"

"Mrs. Jacobsen, Noelle's former owner, is letting me stay here. Let's just say that my apartment with no yard didn't suit her." That was the understatement of the century.

"Malamutes like to have room to run. Did she destroy anything?"

"Couch. Shoes."

He chuckled.

Before she could analyze her reasoning or stop herself, she asked, "If the dog is eating chicken and rice, would you like to have that for dinner? Maybe arroz con pollo for the humans?"

The man grinned, and it hit her in the chest. In an earlier era, she would have fanned herself to cool down.

"I would appreciate that. My cooking skills are enough that I can survive, but they haven't progressed much beyond that point."

Molly laughed. "Then sit down and relax."

"I'll sit beside Noelle while you cook. I think she's enjoying being petted right now."

Molly's breath hitched as she watched him do that, her dog sighing as he rubbed by her ears.

Walking toward the kitchen, she asked, "Do I need to know anything special about Noelle's chicken."

"Boil it in water with no seasonings or other additions to it."

"Yuck!" Molly searched through the cupboards for the right sizes of pans. "I'm glad I asked because I would have at least added salt and pepper."

When Noelle still didn't want to get up by the time the humans had finished dinner, Joe knelt next to her and examined her further. "I still believe my diagnosis is correct, but I think I should stay and watch her for a while, just to be sure. If I had my clinic open, I would have had her stay the night."

Molly gasped. What he wasn't saying was making her nervous. Was it worse than she'd realized? This also created a new problem: she had to spend more time alone with Joe. The last thing she wanted was alone time that could lead to another Christmas romance.

Dinner passed quickly because she'd been so distracted by Noelle that she'd said little. She carried their dishes into the kitchen. "We could watch a movie, I guess. Unless, of course, you have somewhere else to be, and you mean you'll watch her for a half hour." The man probably had a wife and three children to get home to.

He sat on the couch. "No. I don't have anything planned for tonight."

She chose a chair. He still hadn't answered her question well enough that she knew his marital status. Ignoring the question of why she cared about that, said, "I was excited when I found out that I get to live here. I've been living alone in a small apartment in town."

There, that should do it.

Joe watched the woman seated across from him. Was she asking if he was single? He certainly wouldn't mind if she was. Up until now, he had gotten the distinct impression that she was anything but interested, and he'd respected her wishes.

"I also have a small apartment in town, a bachelor pad." Could he be any clearer than that? "I took the first place I saw with the plan to choose my long-term home once I knew the area better."

"I'm saving for a house, so cheapest won for me." Molly smiled. Every time she did that, his heart raced. "As a vet, I'm sure you have many pets and were able to find a pet-friendly apartment. Noelle and I had to move in a hurry when I discovered my place was *not*."

He pictured his sweet golden retriever, Millie. "I lost my dog not long before I moved here. Most vets have multiple cats, dogs, and anything else that comes along, but I had so much schoolwork followed by long hours of work that I didn't think it would be fair to them. I moved to Alaska alone." He felt like brushing his hands together for emphasis.

"Let's choose a movie. Mrs. Jacobsen has a large library, probably because she doesn't have cable out here."

His interest in Molly meant he had to tell her *where* his practice would be located—and before someone else told her. He suspected that she wouldn't be happy with him no matter how she found out. "Molly, have you heard where my new vet office will be?"

"Not yet. I'm surprised that piece of gossip hasn't come to the bakery yet. I usually get all the news early." She glanced back at him and held up a DVD. "Does this look good?"

Barely glancing at it, he said, "Sure. I'm moving into Aimee's space."

She froze with the disc in her hand. "You're the one? Why didn't you say something earlier?"

"Because I knew you would be upset."

She slid the movie into the player. "You were wise. I would have been indignant for Aimee's sake, but it turned out that she's happy to be closing earlier than she'd expected." She stood. "Can I get you a soda or hot chocolate before I start the movie?"

"Hot chocolate would be great." As she did that, he really noticed his surroundings for the first time. When he'd arrived, his focus had been on the dog.

A huge tree dominated the room. Turning, he found decorations in every possible nook and cranny. "Are you a fan of Christmas?"

A chuckle came from the kitchen. "Mrs. Jacobsen must be. She decorated before she left." After a slight pause, he heard, "Oh, no!"

He jumped to his feet. "Are you okay?"

Molly stepped out of the kitchen carrying two mugs. "Joe, I just realized that I have to take all of these decorations down!"

He wanted to offer to help, but he wasn't sure how she'd respond. Instead, he took one of the mugs from her and returned to the couch.

Molly frowned as she sat. "Aimee and Jack will help. My parents too." She pushed play on the remote, and the movie began.

Joe stared at the TV screen for a solid ten minutes of the movie before he paid enough attention to notice what it was. He'd been so worried about the earlier conversation that he hadn't noticed Molly had held up a romantic comedy.

About halfway through the movie, Noelle stood and wobbled over to the door, where she whined, wanting to go out. Molly blinked and rubbed her eyes. She must have fallen asleep.

He said, "I'll take her out."

Molly blinked and yawned. "I've been putting the leash on her after dark, but I don't think she's going to go too far tonight."

"Agreed." He walked over and opened the door for Noelle. She slowly went down the steps, did her business, and returned at the same speed. He hoped Noelle was doing better than she looked. After closing the door, Joe turned around, and found Molly sound asleep in her chair with her head leaning to the side.

"Molly, you seem to need to get to bed."

She opened her eyes again, and her head bobbed as she fought nodding off again. "I'm sorry. Bakers get an early start. I'm not used to late nights."

He chuckled. "It's 9 o'clock."

"See, I told you. I'm usually in bed by eight." She looked over at Noelle with concern in her eyes. "I'm willing to stay up all night, though, if that's what we need to do. Either that or you're welcome to spend the night here." Her eyes widened as she quickly added, "In one of the many bedrooms in this large house."

"I knew that's what you meant. I'll take you up on that offer. I can get up several times in the night to check on Noelle. Do you make breakfast for yourself when you get up in the morning?" He hoped she'd say yes so he'd have two delicious meals in a row.

"I just go into my bakery and eat one of my day-old pastries, which are still great."

"Too bad." He snapped his fingers. When he did that, Noelle looked up at him with a little more interest. Maybe she was coming out of it. "I was about to tell you how I liked my eggs."

Molly raised an eyebrow. "You're welcome to use the kitchen."

He grinned and followed her down the hallway.

"This is my room." She pointed to one on the left. "But there are three other bedrooms. The one next door has its own bath too." She pointed down the hall to the left.

"I'm going to feel like I'm in a fancy bed-and-breakfast."

She rolled her eyes. "To complete that picture, if you're willing to get up at four, I may be able to make you some breakfast."

"Deal."

When she walked into her room and turned around, she gave him one last smile before closing her door.

She was one of the kindest women he had met in a long time. That touched him more than if she were a raving beauty. Not that she wasn't pretty. With her blonde hair in a ponytail, she was, but in a very girl-next-door way.

He laughed to himself as he entered his room. For tonight, she *was* the girl next door.

CHAPTER EIGHT

Two days after Noelle's problem, she was back to her old, running self. Molly's old couch now rested in peace at the dump, and she had fully moved into her new home.

For a much-needed break after her many recent problems, she and Aimee walked from her bakery to a clothing store down the street to do a little shopping for her friend's honeymoon. With Molly's mother on duty at the bakery, and having just returned from a run home to let the dog out, she had a moment for girly fun.

When they slowed down to look at the new sign over Joe's clinic, he waved them inside.

"I'd like your opinions. I think I'll paint the walls a vibrant color. Maybe a nice blue. Do you know anyone who can draw an animal like a cat or dog on the wall? Something—and I hesitate to use this word—cute."

Aimee and Molly watched him with amusement and

Aimee answered. "I'm surprised to find myself saying this, because you're the one pushing me out before Christmas—"

Joe winced.

"—but I'm a good artist. That's part of my work. I draw jewelry, but I can also draw a cat or a dog. Both if you'd like."

"That would be great! If you only have time to do the outline, I should be able to fill it in. I don't have much income right now as I'm setting up my practice, but I'll treat your cat or dog for free."

"I don't have either right now. Maybe once Jack and I are married and we move into a place of our own. I'm engaged."

She held her left hand up. The ring was a unique design of interlocking swirls of yellow gold with diamonds in and around them.

"I'm a guy, but even I can tell that's beautiful."

She got a dreamy expression as she looked at her hand. "I'm really happy with how the design came out. I envisioned it as abstract hearts linked together. The wedding band will be snugged up next to it."

Joe stared at her hand. "If you have enough talent to do that, you can certainly draw animals on this wall. My life in Homer is coming together nicely."

"As soon as your walls are painted the color you want, let me know. Oh, and our friend Molly here is an excellent painter. She helped me paint these walls when I moved in."

An air of matchmaking filled the room. Molly glared at her friend.

He must have noticed her expression because he added, "I'm sure I can take care of it myself or find someone else to help. Don't worry about it."

Molly sighed. "Aimee's right. I like painting. But it'll have to be on Sunday when I'm not open or after three in the afternoon."

"Okay, and I will treat Noelle for free for the next year. How does that sound?"

"I have no idea what you're getting yourself into, but that's a deal I can't turn down."

And so it was that Molly found herself with a paint roller in one hand and a tray of vibrant blue paint in front of her a few days later. Noelle was safely tied up in the back with a chew bone to keep her happy.

Joe had come to the bakery every morning since their night caring for Noelle. Clearly new to do-it-yourself projects, he'd asked her to give him a list of things to buy for their painting day.

Aimee claimed she wasn't trying to push her and Joe together. Molly wasn't sure she believed her friend. Oh, she knew that Aimee wouldn't lie to her. But one person's helping a friend was another person's matchmaking.

This afternoon, she had found Joe inside her friend's former business with a couple of gallons of paint, two paint rollers, and trays—exactly as she'd directed. She hadn't thought of a tarp, but he'd spread one over the entire floor. *That was probably a good plan,* she thought when she took in his bewildered expression. She explained how to roll the paint on in a W and then fill in the area.

As he put his paint roller in the paint-filled tray for the first time, she said, "You have me for two hours and then I have to go back and mix up some cookie dough so it can chill overnight."

Joe lifted his roller and stopped with it in midair.

"You're dripping!"

"I'm glad I bought the tarp." He put the roller to the wall and did as she'd explained, with good results. He might actually become a decent painter.

"Molly, if you truly don't have time, don't feel like you have to help me."

She rolled the wall and then dipped the roller back in to refill it. "You're doing me a favor of sorts. I feel like I've been spending every spare minute either in the bakery, or in the van running back and forth between the bakery and home to let Noelle out, something I do when my mom comes in to work every day. Then I hurry home again after closing. Having her in the back with us is actually a good thing." She sighed. "I'm still figuring out how to care for a dog." She swiped at hair that had fallen in her face.

"I can help."

"You've already done so much for her."

"Molly, you're painting my walls right now."

"I know, but—"

"I have the solution. You're helping me. What if I trade you dog care lessons for the help you're giving me?"

A handsome veterinarian helping her learn to care for Noelle? She may not be interested in dating him, but she couldn't say she wouldn't appreciate the lessons. "I'd like to say yes, but I'm only painting. You're already treating her for free for a year."

"I'd like to help you."

Glancing over at him, she wondered why. His face appeared flushed like he was embarrassed. Maybe he didn't want a dog to suffer at the hands of incompetence.

"I accept your offer."

"And she can stay here with me while you work after you're done. I don't think I'll be getting out of here early tonight. I'd love to be able to open up in a couple of weeks. By the first of the year, for sure. My parents will be visiting either at Christmas or just after, so I want to be open by then. I guess I want them to see that I've succeeded in life."

He stopped talking and turned a vibrant shade of red. He'd probably opened up more about his family than he'd intended to. Maybe he'd relax if she took the conversation away from his feelings.

"My mother helps me at the bakery. Does your family have any interest in your work?"

He laughed, so her plan worked. "I think I mentioned earlier that my dad's a physician. He's a bit intense some-times, but we get along well. I don't see him working on animals in his spare time. My mother is the college English professor students love, but has little interest in what I do."

Joe dipped his roller in the paint, and held it up, dripping on the floor again. He groaned and put the roller to the wall. "Can you tell that you're needed on this project of mine? It's a fair trade. You help me get my place open by the first of the year, and I teach you what you need to know to have a happy and healthy dog."

How could she turn down that offer? Her attention went to an area where trickles of paint ran down the wall. She went over to him and rolled that area before it could dry. "I think you do need me." As soon as she'd said those words, she wanted to take them back. She turned to face him, not realizing they were only a couple of feet apart, and that made her words even more embarrassing. Her face hot, she said, "I mean—"

He tucked her hair behind her ear, and her heart flip flopped. "I know what you meant. I think we'll be able to work well together."

Molly hurried back to the wall she'd been painting. What they said about nice guys was wrong. She found them much too appealing. Not only did she not have time for romance, but her heart couldn't take another beating.

CHAPTER NINE

*J*oe looked around at his new clinic. Aimee's brothers-in-law had been in Homer last weekend. Molly had talked them into helping him frame and drywall the three exam rooms at the right side of the room. He was always amazed at how easy someone could make a job look when they were really good at it.

He'd divided the back area into an office—which they had also sectioned off for him—and a surgery area. This building wasn't the biggest place in Homer that he could have chosen, but he was still glad that he had picked it. It was centrally located. And having his favorite baker so close was a definite perk.

Molly had agreed to dog lessons. Maybe she'd become more interested in him if they spent time together. She seemed anything but interested right now. He'd been so busy with school for years that he'd barely had time to date. Now he wanted the whole picture of a home and a special woman. Molly could be that woman.

To prevent pushing her further away, he'd just be a friend for now. But he had a plan. He put the first step of that plan in place by texting her to schedule a lesson. She agreed to that afternoon.

She arrived with Noelle on a leash.

"Have you taken her to the beach?" he asked.

She shook her head. "I walked her near where I lived. I didn't take her any farther."

"Then we, my student, are on our way to the Homer Spit."

Noelle danced around.

"She seems to know what that means. Whether or not she likes walking on the beach, I know I always do. Let's go."

Just a few minutes later, they were all loaded into his truck and going down the road, with Noelle alternating between breathing down his neck and putting her nose out the window. It was a little slice of heaven and only got better when the sun peeked through the clouds. Even with the sunshine, the window's air had a bite to it.

"I hadn't thought about it being too cold and frozen to take a walk."

Molly rolled her window down a crack. "It's cold—but not as cold as a lot of Alaska—and it's damp here in the winter because we're on the water. As long as I'm bundled up in a heavy coat, gloves, and hat, I love walking on the beach." She breathed deeply. "And the scent of the ocean."

It seemed as though he'd chosen well for the first activity.

They drove through town and down the road to the Spit. Every time he thought about the word "spit," he was caught between a chuckle and a grimace. But, for some strange reason, that was what this piece of geography was known as.

"Drive to the end, and I'll show you where to park."

He did as instructed, and Molly pointed toward a parking lot.

When he stopped, she turned in her seat and clipped the leash on Noelle. "I've watched people run their dogs up and down the beach all of my life."

He heard a wistful tone in her voice, probably the same one that had gotten her the dog in the first place.

"Why didn't you get a dog as soon as you were on your own?"

She popped the door open and climbed out. "I didn't want to have to shut a dog up in an apartment while I was gone for hours every day. I'm still not super happy about leaving her home alone a lot, but I will make it work. For right now, she has so much room to run at Mrs. Jacobsen's when I'm there that she's a very happy dog."

She let Noelle out and the dog pranced around, clearly excited about her outing.

Sighing, she continued, "I'm just not sure how much house I'm going to be able to afford when I buy one. I think getting any yard will be a bonus for my first home."

They walked toward the salt water. This water was a

bit gray, but it lapped on the shore and carried the mysterious scent of the sea that had lured men to her all through time.

The dog pulled ahead, and Molly leaped forward with Noelle racing toward the surf.

Molly yelled, "How do I stop her?"

He knew this dog was well trained. "Noelle, stop!"

The dog ground to a halt and dropped her rump onto the rocky ground.

Molly stood next to her, panting.

"Let's call that lesson number one. Noelle clearly loves being here. There's no one else out here right now. You should be able to unclip her leash and let her run. I'm going to warn you in advance, though," he added, as Molly leaned down and gave the dog her freedom, "that she will probably have a belly covered in sand, and she's going to smell like the sea."

Molly laughed as the dog splashed in the water and barked at an incoming wave. "I don't care. She looks like she's having fun already. You can show me how to give her a bath later. Let's call that lesson number two." She spun around toward him. "I'm so sorry. I have no right to take this much of your time. I'll figure out how to give her a bath on my own."

Not only did he think that trying to get a big, exuberant dog into a tub would be difficult, but keeping her there would be even harder. Besides, not helping would mean losing another chance to spend time with her. "No, this is my day off. Let's just have fun. We'll do Dog Bathing 101 later."

She grinned at him and laughed as Noelle raced up and down the beach in front of them. Joe stood beside her and wondered if her agreeing to their plan was simply a means to a goal or if she had some interest in him.

"What's that?" he asked as he pointed across the bay, and casually—he hoped—put his hand on her shoulder.

"That direction is Kachemak Bay State Park." When she leaned into his warmth, he closed his eyes.

This wasn't one-sided. He had a chance with her.

Joe leaned down to pick up a stick and immediately regretted it when he lost the warmth of her touch. Noelle raced over to him and dug in her back feet as she came to a halt, her eyes focused on the stick.

He threw it, and they began a game of fetch as she chased it and returned it to him. They played until his arm was sore and the dog looked like she was winding down.

Molly wrapped her arms around herself and shivered.

"Noelle, let's go home." He knelt, and the dog came to him.

Molly looked around as though she'd lost track of where she was. "Thank you for bringing me here. It was great for her, and I needed to just be outside and relax. This"— she gestured toward the water and the mountains —"is why I choose to make Alaska, and especially Homer, my home."

"It does take your breath away, doesn't it?"

She looked at him as though he had said the right thing. That he understood.

He asked her, "Did you go out on the water often when you were growing up?"

They walked toward the car, Noelle once again leashed beside Molly but now with much-diminished energy. "Aimee's grandparents own a fishing charter company, and we'd go out a lot when she was here." Molly looked up at him. "She didn't live in Homer year round. My parents didn't own a boat, but we frequently fished from shore."

Molly focused ahead and picked her way over the rocks. "Now, Aimee takes me out on one of the boats, and we have a lot of fun. A few months ago, she captained one, and a group of us went for a hike from Halibut Cove Lagoon." She pointed across the bay.

"I don't know what's there, but it sounds like fun. Do people go out on the water much here in the winter?"

"There are some places where you wouldn't want to go if they had iced up. But for the most part, sure. Maybe I can talk Aimee into taking us out sometime soon. Would that be a good lesson for Noelle? How to be on a boat safely?"

"I think we'd better get a few more lessons under our belt so I understand how she reacts in different situations. And we would get a dog life jacket for her in case she did fall in."

Molly's eyes widened as she heard those words. "I hadn't even thought of that. Maybe this is a bad idea all around."

"No, it's not. You live next to the water, so there's no reason you shouldn't be able to enjoy it with her. We just need to take precautions as we would if she were a small child." A seagull swooped down toward them. Noelle bounced on her feet and howled at it. He added, "Just like she acts like a small child sometimes."

Molly laughed, and he joined in.

"My big, furry child."

He was glad to hear the way that she was speaking about her dog. It showed she had accepted Noelle as hers and that they would find a way to make their life together work. He needed to help them. If it just so happened that he helped her fall for him, he had this feeling deep inside his heart that they'd find a way to make that work too.

CHAPTER TEN

 olly sat, staring straight ahead as he drove. So much for her promise to herself of not chasing a man. He'd simply rested his hand on her shoulder, and she'd leaned into it like a teenager. Humiliation washed through her. She knew her face was burning bright red from the heat it was giving off. He was simply the helpful new veterinarian in town. She needed to remember that.

The man loved dogs. The man had not shown any special interest in her. Just Noelle.

"Has the Christmas season been busy for you so far in the bakery?"

Business. She could talk about business all day and keep the discussion away from anything too personal.

"We have been busy. I recently hired a college student who's home for the holidays to help." Molly had taken a small hit to her budget, but she'd woken up this morning looking forward to the day instead of feeling over-whelmed. "It takes quite a bit of juggling from Thanks-giving on to make sure I get all the orders taken care of."

"Orders? Do you mean to take care of the customers in your café?"

"No. Well, there are those customers too. But I was talking about the mail orders. I ship cookies anywhere in the state. There are quite a few places that don't have a bakery or anything close to a bakery. My cookies go everywhere from Eagle to Adak."

"The way you said that with pride makes me think those are towns that are far apart from each other."

Molly laughed. "I forget sometimes that you're new to our state. Eagle is a small place up on the Yukon River, not too far from the Canadian border. It's in a gold-mining area, and the road closes in the winter, so for months you can only fly in or out or have a very long ride on a snow-mobile—if there was some reason you chose to leave. And Adak is down deep in the Aleutian Islands and about as far from Anchorage as it is from New York City to Dallas, Texas. There isn't too much going on when you're that remote from civilization, but some hardy souls call it home. The orders come in on my website or on the phone."

"Then how were you able to paint my clinic and go to the beach?"

"I had thought I could get along a little longer without extra help, but our furry friend in the backseat taught me that I was wrong. That's why I hired the student."

"Dogs are good like that. They teach us to enjoy life more."

Molly was about to argue the point, that she hadn't meant that. When she took a moment to think about it, though, he was right. Noelle had helped her slow down and enjoy the season more.

As they spoke, Noelle started what Joe called "talking" and made *woo-woo* sounds. Molly had thought every dog simply barked. Apparently, malamutes were not like other dogs.

"Are you making good progress on your veterinary office?"

He grimaced, and she regretted her question.

"Never mind. None of my business."

He turned onto the road that led to Mrs. Jacobsen's house, Molly's new residence. "It isn't that. It's that I keep fighting delays in shipping to Alaska with my equipment."

Molly did her best to stifle a chuckle.

Apparently, she failed because he asked, "Okay, what's funny about that?"

"Shipping to Alaska is often problematic. It's best to laugh about it. Aimee's grandparents talk about what it was like when they first moved into the area. And a friend of theirs talked about living in Anchorage in the 1950s. Everything, including eggs, came up slowly on a ship. He had to crack each one carefully to see if he had an edible or rotten egg."

"That sounds bad. So I guess this is considered an improvement?"

Molly laughed. "A big improvement. But every once in a while people still have to argue that Alaska is not a foreign country when they want something shipped here."

"You're kidding?"

"Absolutely not. Aimee's grandparents also mentioned that they had taken a trip to London years ago, and while they were talking to someone from the East Coast—New York, I think—the woman asked what kind of money we used in Alaska."

Joe grinned. "I must admit that it does feel like you're in another country when you're here. It isn't just the distance, but that does play into it. Every once in a while, I feel like I'm living on an island, and that starts to concern me. But then I look at the natural beauty around me, and I realize that I probably can't explore everywhere in Alaska that I would want to in a lifetime, and the feeling goes away."

This man had a way of tugging at her heartstrings with how he saw her world. "You're right. I've lived here my whole life, and I still find new places to go."

They pulled up in front of the house. Molly got out and opened the door for Noelle, who raced out of the vehicle and danced around the front yard as though saying, "We made it back. I'm so glad I'm here."

Molly laughed as she went toward the front door with Joe and Noelle following behind her. By the time Molly got there, Noelle already had her nose pressed against the door. Molly would have to take this lesson to heart and run her on the beach more often if it made her ready to rest.

When the dog started to dart through the door as she opened it, Joe grabbed her collar. "No, you don't. We need to get you cleaned up before you bring all that sand into the house."

Noelle looked up at him with her bright, curious eyes fixed on his face.

"Grab her brush, Molly. Let's see if we can brush out her belly before we let her inside. In the summer, I would suggest using the hose, but it's way too cold for that."

Every time Molly reached out with the brush, Noelle nuzzled her and licked her hand. She finally ended up giving up, sitting on the porch and brushing Noelle with her arms around her.

"Okay, I think that's as good as it gets," Joe said. "My guess is that there's one bathroom in particular that Mrs. Jacobsen used to wash her dog. These dogs are fur machines, and we don't want to clog the drain. Have you noticed one that has a mesh strainer in it to catch hair?"

"I've never in my life checked showers for strainers."

They stepped inside the door, and Molly said, "Noelle, sit!" The dog did as she was told. She had a feeling that an untrained malamute could be a nightmare with all of their energy and strength. Fortunately, this one had been well trained.

Joe returned seconds later. "The hall bath looks like it's been set up with her things. There are some large towels in the closet that I suspect are for Noelle. I pulled one out that had a beach umbrella on it, and there isn't much beach umbrella time in Alaska."

She clipped the leash on Noelle, and they went down the hall together. When they got to the bathroom door, the dog plunked her bottom on the floor and stopped. Molly tugged on the leash, but she refused to move.

"Are you coming in here?" Joe called out from the bathroom.

"The dog is staging a sit-down protest."

He peered around the corner, looked at Noelle, and grinned. "That's both good and bad. She's a smart dog because she knows this is where she goes to get a bath."

"But that's also bad because she knows this is where she goes to get a bath."

"Exactly." He laughed.

Molly tugged on the leash. Nothing happened, except the dog may have steeled her muscles tighter.

Joe said, "Now I understand the jar of treats with the towels and hair dryer."

Four treats later, the dog stood in the tub. She was soon clean.

Once they'd toweled her off in the tub, they had her jump out, and Molly started blowing her dry. If someone had told her two weeks ago that she would be blow drying *her dog*, she would have said that would be impossible.

When Molly finished, she put her arms around Noelle's neck and hugged her. "That's a good dog."

The dog howled. She wouldn't move, even when they opened the bathroom door.

"Any idea what's wrong, Joe? She doesn't seem to want to go anywhere."

Joe grabbed the canister of treats out of the closet. "I have a feeling that she gets another treat for being a good girl."

He held it down, and the dog snapped it up, then stood and trotted out the bathroom door and into the hall, where she stopped and sat down again.

"And we have to go through this ordeal every time I walk her on the beach?"

"Every time she gets sand covering her belly. You could probably walk her higher on the beach and keep her out of the water. At least you could try to do that."

Molly pictured Noelle running and playing as the waves hit the shore, and she knew that was highly unlikely. "I guess I just need to get better at baths and become proficient at doing it all by myself."

The thought of doing all of that alone saddened her, which seemed odd because she'd been alone for a lot of things in her life. She'd started her business on her own. Having Joe around seemed to make even everyday events more fun, though. *But we aren't dating. He's helping me.*

Gathering the supplies, Joe reached for the treat jar. Molly took a step backward to give him enough room to move, and her foot caught in the bath towel. Arms flailing, she tried to find something to grab a hold of so she didn't fall face forward into the sink. Joe dropped what he'd been holding and grabbed her arms to stabilize her.

"I've got you."

Molly looked up into his eyes and realized that he did have her. Somehow, she'd become more interested in this man than she should. Looking into his eyes, she sighed.

He leaned toward her, and she moved forward.

Was he about to kiss her? Did she *want* him to do that? She slid her hands up his arms to his shoulders. Strong shoulders. Working as a veterinarian apparently took some muscle.

Time moved slowly. She could feel his breath mingling with hers as he leaned forward. When his lips were almost touching hers, Noelle howled, and they both jumped back.

He reached for the wet towel. "Um, let me put these things away."

"Good idea. I'm going to go check on Noelle to see if everything's okay." Molly rushed out the door. Oh, she expected Noelle to be fine. But if she stuck around, she might have to decide if she had liked whatever had just happened.

She found the dog quietly sitting in front of the window. Molly reached down to pet her head. "That's a good dog. You knew what you were doing, didn't you?"

The dog chattered.

CHAPTER ELEVEN

*J*oe leaned against the bathroom wall. He was interested in Molly. Of course, he wanted to kiss her. But she was so skittish that he felt like he would chase her away forever if he wasn't careful with her. Sure, she'd put her hands on his arms when he'd leaned in for the kiss, but she'd also run out of the room as fast as she could seconds later.

He wanted to pursue his interest in her, but he knew he had to wait until she showed interest in him before he did anything more than help her with her dog. He just hoped he was strong enough for that. He'd come to Homer hoping to find his forever home, but he hadn't realized that he needed more than just a new vet clinic. He and the baker made a sweet couple.

A sound from Noelle brought him back to the present. He cleared the drain of the volume of fur he had expected and went down the hall, where he found the two of them standing side by side at the front window. They were a cute pair. Molly clearly hadn't realized how much she needed Noelle in her life.

He pulled his phone out of his pocket and snapped a photo. He'd show it to her later tonight.

"It's all tidied up and ready for her next bath."

Noelle turned toward him and did her whimper-howling sound as though to argue that she didn't need baths.

He and Molly both laughed.

Molly seemed nervous as she stood there. Was it because of their almost-kiss?

"I have plenty of food, if you would like to stay for dinner."

He didn't want to sound too eager. "What are you making?"

"Mrs. Jacobsen said to use whatever I found in the freezer. I discovered some halibut dated from this summer. I thought I would pair that with a salad and some roasted potatoes." She still had the hesitant tone in her voice, and he wasn't sure why. Had he blown it with her?

"That sounds delicious. Thank you for the invitation."

At that, she let out a big sigh and smiled at him. She'd seemed worried that he would say no. Maybe he had a chance with her.

"You can entertain Noelle while I cook dinner."

Or she simply needed a dog sitter. Back to square one.

"That sounds like a fair arrangement. I do have enough skills to help cook, though, if you want me to."

"I actually think it might be best if you kept her busy. I'm still not used to having a dog underfoot. I almost tripped over her while I made dinner last night."

About forty-five minutes later, after having played with the ball *and* a pull toy, Noelle was curled up on her bed when Molly announced, "Dinner will be ready in just a few minutes. Would you like to set the table?"

"I can do that."

Molly added that he should open cupboards and look for whatever it was that he wanted. "I'm still not sure where everything is myself."

He did as he was told and found the plates, silverware, and napkins. As he put a napkin at each place, the lights flickered, dimmed, and went out.

"Joe?"

"I'm over here by the table. Do you know where there are candles or flashlights or anything to give us light?"

"I don't, and I certainly should. Someone who considers herself an Alaskan and didn't think ahead enough for emergency supplies should lose that title. It's not like we're strangers to power outages, especially when living away from town."

He pulled his phone out of his pocket and put it on flashlight mode. "There were many things neatly organized in that closet where I found bath supplies. I'll check there."

"If you don't find it, would you grab my purse, which is

on the table by the door on your way back? Then I can at least have a flashlight."

He found battery-powered lanterns, candle holders, and a box with candles. "We're set for light. But I just realized, is dinner ruined?"

She laughed. "Leave it to a man to think about his stomach. No. Everything was ready. I was about to put the potatoes in a serving bowl."

He set the candelabra he'd found on the dining room table and lit three candles in it. That would probably provide more than enough light for them to eat by. As soon as he had done that, he stepped back in amazement. The flickering light of the candles reflecting off the plates and the silverware had turned a simple meal into something much more romantic. When he turned toward Molly, and discovered she was also fixated on the scene, he suspected he wasn't the only one who thought that. Maybe a power outage was exactly what they needed.

"Let's serve ourselves here in the kitchen. I've already tripped once today, so let's not make it twice." As soon as Molly said those words, she realized that her memory was of her practically falling into his arms. *Don't chase a man* was still the best policy from her experience. Men clearly did not enjoy being pursued.

When she heard footsteps, she pictured Joe crowded

beside her as he served himself. "If you don't mind, I can just put our food on the plates myself."

He pulled out a chair and sat at the table. "I'm going to be right here and not in your way. Oh, and if that wonderful scent is of roasted potatoes with herbs, you can give me an extra portion of those, please."

"Consider it done. There's something comforting about these particular potatoes on a cold day. I'm going to make beef stew tomorrow."

"Sounds delicious," Joe said as she carried his plate toward the table. She watched him as he stopped, realizing what he'd said. "Not that I'm inviting myself, of course. It just sounds good."

Molly didn't say anything because now she was caught in a conundrum. If she invited the man to dinner, was she chasing him? She'd wait and see how the rest of the evening went.

He took a bite of the halibut, closed his eyes, and sighed. "This is delicious." Then he tasted the potatoes, which were crispy on the outside, soft inside, and sprinkled with herbs. "Heavenly."

"Even if you're not a salad guy, give the salad a try. It has homemade dressing."

"Dating a woman who owns a bakery and restaurant is a really fine idea."

She froze with a fork full of food in front of her mouth.

He sat back in his seat. "Not that we're dating. I'm just

saying that it would be a good idea." He looked heaven-ward as though he hoped for divine intervention.

Molly felt her skin flush from the praise. At least that was what she told herself. His words about dating had nothing to do with her. She changed the subject. "If every-thing goes according to my plan, I'll be out of the bakery by about three tomorrow—if you need any more help with your painting or projects." That was being helpful. That wasn't being pushy and throwing yourself at a man. Neighborly. That would be her new policy with Joe. Neighborly.

He returned to eating. "I just have the outline on the wall of the animals that Aimee sketched out for me. I need to fill it in, and then most of the painting will be done. I am on track to open if and when my equipment and supplies arrive."

Molly swallowed her bite of potatoes. "I can help with the painting."

His gaze narrowed. "Will you be better at it than I am? I thought I could do it, but now that I've seen how profes-sional the outline is . . ."

"Of course I will. I painted the walls. *We* painted the walls."

"But this is different. I was thinking I might have to find someone to fill it in. Aimee said she had some projects to finish up for Christmas gifts, or she would do it."

Molly said, "That's true. Christmas is far busier for her than it is for me at the bakery because she can spend an entire week on a single custom jewelry piece. She has quite a few of them that she's been fortunate to get commissions for, including a wedding set from a couple who was referred to her by another customer a few months ago."

She held up her hand and moved it as though she were writing. "Remember, I decorate cakes. Picture me writing 'Happy Birthday' on a cake. Steady hand. I can certainly fill in paint in the shape of the cat and dog that are already on the wall."

He blew out a big sigh. "Then I thank you. I don't seem to have any skills when it comes to the arts. I'm 100 percent science."

"And my only science is baking. I have to understand some basics so that I can get bread to rise and not be a doorstop and cakes to be fluffy and not discs that could be thrown for Noelle to fetch." She grinned and put another bite of food in her mouth.

He asked, "What's your favorite kind of cake?"

Molly answered. "Angel food," and that started a chain of questions and answers between them that lasted for over an hour. The conversation was easy and smooth. She could have said that she'd never enjoyed a date more. But this wasn't a date. This was dinner with a friend. Yes, that was what it was.

"Should I pick up Noelle to take her to your clinic? Or should I just come home, let her out, and leave her in the house?"

"Molly, there's one thing that you need to learn about

almost all vets. The more animals there are, the better the day is. Go ahead and bring her."

As Molly carried her plate to the kitchen, being careful not to trip over unseen obstacles, the power came back on. "That was short." *Just long enough to have us eating by candlelight.* "You've still got your phone out, Joe. What day is this?"

"Sunday. I know that without looking."

"No, silly. I mean, what's the date?"

"The twelfth."

"Then it's time for the lighting of Homer's Christmas tree tomorrow night. I always go."

Noelle wandered into the room, and did her talking sound. This dog was so cute. Big and quite furry, but so cute.

"What do you say, girl? Do you want to go see the tree lighting?"

Noelle chattered again.

Molly set the plate down on the counter. Then she whirled around to face Joe again. "*Can* I go with her?"

His brow furrowed. "Do you need tickets or something? Is that what you're asking?"

"No, I was wondering if I can take her into a group of people."

"Well, my guess is that you can. There's nothing about a malamute that says they hate people. And she didn't growl at me or Aimee. Let's put her in a harness that's very secure, and we'll be careful not to stand too close to anyone so we can get a feel for what she's like in a group."

"Lesson number three?"

"That sounds like a plan."

Molly turned to face the kitchen so Joe wouldn't see the grin on her face. *Not a date. Just helping with the dog.* She needed to say those words to herself throughout the day tomorrow instead of being excited about a date.

He pushed back from the table and stood. "Do you need help with the dishes?"

Molly had never had a man ask that before. It was unfortunate that she really didn't. Having him stand beside her would have been very nice. "In my apartment, I would have said wholeheartedly yes. But here, it doesn't matter. I have a dishwasher now." She proudly folded down the door of the appliance. "It's a beautiful thing after living without one for years. At home, that is. I, of course, have a dishwasher at the bakery."

"Then, I think I'll say good night and be on my way. I will meet you at my clinic tomorrow afternoon. And I'll have the paint and brushes ready."

Molly had hoped he'd stay a little longer. She pictured them standing on the front porch as she sent him on his way for the evening with a smile—and him kissing her. "I'm not sleepy." It must have been the thought that made her brain go that direction because she yawned and covered her mouth. "I thought I was okay, but maybe I do need to make sure I get enough sleep." If he left now while she did the dishes, though, she wouldn't find out if she did want him to kiss her goodnight.

"You did say you were usually in bed by 8:00 p.m., and we're right about there."

She sighed. "So we are. Then bye." She gave a little wave from where she was in the kitchen.

Noelle looked from her to Joe and howled.

That pretty much summed up how Molly felt about the situation. Instead of sitting beside Joe on the couch with romance in the air, she was up to her elbows in dirty dishes, and he was on his way to the door by himself.

"I'll let myself out then. Have a good evening, Molly."

"You too," she called out and then heard the door click shut behind him.

CHAPTER TWELVE

*M*olly loved her bakery. She really did. She loved every part of it. The pink aprons she'd chosen. The paper doilies she put under the baked goods. In a state where things often looked woodsy, she had gone for a traditional bakery look that leaned a little toward the feminine. The doily caught her eye again. Maybe a lot toward the feminine. None of the men who came in seemed to mind. As long as she fed them cinnamon rolls and other baked goods they enjoyed, they didn't appear to care in the slightest.

But every moment of this particular day, from the wee hours of the morning when she'd come in and flipped on the lights to this moment when the lunch crowd was gone and only a few stragglers were having a second cup of coffee, all she could think about was going to Joe's clinic this afternoon.

Her temporary employee had grown up baking with

her mother, so she'd taken to baking here like a pro. With prep work for tomorrow done, Molly grabbed her coat, put on the boots she'd worn to be warm during tonight's tree lighting, and headed down the sidewalk to see Joe, only to find the clinic dark inside. She knocked on the door and peered through the glass, but no one was there.

Molly stepped back and considered what to do. She'd only stopped by to see if it was safe for Noelle before she ran out to get her.

Well, she might have stopped by to see him too.

Maybe she should call Aimee and see if she wanted to go to the tree lighting tonight if Joe had forgotten about her so easily.

Molly hurried to her van, which was parked not far from the bakery, and drove home. With Noelle loaded in the van, she drove off with the dog panting and howling intermittently. Sometimes it was just chatter, that thing she did that had a way of making Molly laugh.

"It may just be you and me solo tonight, Noelle. I'm not sure what's happened with Joe."

When she pulled up in a parking space in front of his clinic, she could tell it was still dark inside. She grabbed her phone to call Aimee to see what she was doing tonight, even though she knew her friend would say she was much too busy to have a night out. A missed call and several missed text messages appeared on her screen. She kept her purse tucked away in her office while she was working, usually remembering to check it occasionally. Not today.

Probably because her head had been so far up in the clouds thinking about this afternoon and tonight. The first text was from Joe.

My equipment arrived!

The excitement popped off the screen. A few minutes later, he had sent another message.

Everything is in Anchorage. Crazy cost to transport to Homer. Need to solve the problem.

A lot less happiness came through this time.

The message after a missed call explained his absence.

I think I can fit it all in my pickup truck. On my way to Anchorage. Hoping I am back for tree lighting.

She checked the time on the texts. They'd all arrived before 9:00 a.m. So he must have already reached Anchorage, loaded his truck, and headed back this way. She hit the call button on her phone.

"Molly, I am so glad you called! I felt like I was standing you up, and I did not want you to think that." His words rushed out as soon as he answered, without giving her a chance to speak first.

"I'm just glad you're okay. I'm sorry I missed all of your attempts to get a hold of me. Where are you now?"

Silence met her question, and she looked at her phone to make sure the call hadn't dropped.

"I'm not sure. I passed somewhere called Cooper Landing not too long ago."

"You made great time!"

"Driving this highway in the middle of the week in December helps. There aren't many vehicles, and the roads are in great condition. The company loaded my freight quickly when I got there too. I think I'm going to be able to make it home in time to go with you tonight."

As much as Molly hated to say it, she replied, "I don't want you to feel like you have to do that. I know you probably want to get the equipment into your clinic tonight."

A rueful laugh came through her phone. "I don't think there's any way for me to do that. If I could just put it in a warm garage for the night, that would help. I don't even like driving it in this much cold, but it is what it is."

The garage at Molly's new home came to mind. "Mrs. Jacobsen's garage is heated, and you're welcome to park there. I know it's silly, but I haven't used it because I've always parked outside. I could drive you home later, and I guess come get you tomorrow at some point to take you to your clinic."

She didn't even want to suggest that he could stay at her house again. That just sounded wrong, no matter how similar the home was to a bed-and-breakfast. Now that she was the teensiest bit interested in him, temptation was just a door away, and she wanted to avoid that.

"That sounds like a great idea. I'll meet you at your place. Then we can go in your van to see the tree lighting tonight. Can we all fit in there?"

Molly laughed. "Sort of. There's a big bench seat, but there will be a large dog sitting in the middle between us. Unless you want to let her sit over by the window. She does love hanging her nose out the window."

CHAPTER THIRTEEN

a couple of hours later, the three of them were packed into the front seat of her van. It was a good thing they'd given Noelle a bath recently, because they were right up next to her, and the doggy smell would have been intense.

"Did you enjoy your drive?"

"I drove through a lot of pretty areas, places I'd like to go back and see, but it all went by in a blur. I'm just thrilled that I have the equipment I wanted. I can now set up my surgery and other parts of my practice."

Molly grimaced. "For some reason, I pictured you handing out pills to dogs and cats. It never occurred to me that you had to operate on them."

"That was one of the things that intrigued me about being a vet. I want to help animals however I can. I wanted to be a doctor like my dad when I was young, but as I got older, it became less about working with people and more about animals."

"Did you have a lot of pets growing up?"

He chuckled. "Mom called it my zoo. She became convinced that when someone didn't want an animal, they would just leave it somewhere in my path. I came home with a puppy. I had a cat follow me into the house. Lizards. You name it, and I probably had it."

"What about a bird?"

He shuddered. "I love all animals, but I'm not as fond of birds. Their bites hurt worse than you can imagine."

Molly found a parking space not too far away from the tree lighting ceremony. "I was reading online today about dog muzzles. Do you think I should get one for her?"

"We'll keep her away from other people and dogs tonight to watch her. That way, she can't get into trouble or hurt anyone. If she looks like she needs one, we'll get it for the next time."

"That makes sense." She clipped Noelle's leash to her harness. "Are you ready to go have some fun, girl?"

The dog talked, and Molly laughed. "I'll take that as a yes."

Joe chuckled. "I agree. That sounded very much like a yes."

The three of them walked down the street from their parking spot to the tree. The closer they got to the tree lighting, the more people they saw. Molly pulled back on the leash. "We'd better slow down and wait for everyone else to choose where they want to stand." She could see at least two other dogs, maybe three if that was a dog tail next to the tree. Noelle must have been able to see them or smell them too, because she let out a howl, and there were a couple of answering barks.

A male voice asked, "Is that Noelle? Are you here, Mrs. Jacobsen?" When a man walking their way stepped under a street light, she saw a vaguely familiar older man. He must come into the bakery sometimes.

"Mrs. Jacobsen moved in with her daughter in Anchorage."

The man knelt down. "But I know this is Noelle." He ruffled the dog's ears, and Noelle seemed to enjoy the attention. She licked across his cheek with her tongue, and he laughed. Standing, he said, "I'm surprised that she left Noelle behind. She loves that dog so much."

"She needed a home for her, and I offered to take her in."

"I wish I'd known. I would have been happy to take her. As you can tell, we've always gotten along well."

Molly sucked in her breath and tugged the leash closer.

Joe must have sensed her panic because he put his arm around her and pulled her to his side.

"We're getting along very well."

"I wonder if I should give her a call. I've always wanted a malamute."

Joe rubbed Molly's upper arm. "I think it's probably too late for that," he said. "Molly and Noelle have become buddies."

The man sighed. "That's too bad, but I'm glad she found a good home."

Molly let out the breath. Smiling genuinely, she said, "This is the first time I've brought her out into a crowd. I wasn't sure how she would do."

The man laughed. "Noelle loves people, especially children. She's a child magnet. Some malamutes I know aren't happy with other animals, but I've never seen Noelle act anything but friendly around other dogs. I know until a year or so ago that Mrs. Jacobsen had a couple of cats. They were senior kitties, and she didn't have any problems between them. There's even one photo I remember her posting to social media of the cats curled up next to Noelle."

Molly grinned. It figured that Mrs. Jacobsen would be on social media. She defied every stereotype of someone her age. It was too bad her daughter hadn't been able to see that.

As the man walked away, a boy who must have been about ten ran up to Noelle. No matter what this man had said about Noelle loving children, Molly felt her heart leap into her throat. When Noelle just gave one of her whining and whimpering sounds as the boy neared her, Molly's panic subsided.

The boy held out his hand so Noelle could sniff it. Then he petted her, and Noelle leaned into it and slowly wagged her tail. The boy ran back to his parents, who waited without concern for him to return. It must be true that Noelle was known for being good with children. Now Molly felt like this evening was going to go well.

At that moment, she realized that Joe had put his arm around her to comfort her a few minutes ago. She'd appreciated it but not quite registered the action. Joe was still holding her close to his side and rubbing her upper arm. It was something she could get used to, but they couldn't stay here all night.

Noelle chose that moment to run around them, circling them with her leash. Molly turned and reached for the dog, but she moved too quickly. She found herself chest to chest with the handsome vet and lashed so tightly to him that they wouldn't be going anywhere until they unraveled this problem.

The dog sat down and looked up at them as if to say, "My work is done here."

Molly closed her eyes for a few seconds. "This is embarrassing."

Joe cleared his throat. "She moved so quickly that I didn't see it coming."

Tilting her head back to speak to him, Molly found herself staring into Joe's eyes. His gaze dropped to her mouth. One kiss couldn't hurt her heart, could it? Could she have a merry Christmas and a little romance?

He leaned in for a kiss. Wrapping her arms around him, she kissed him back. She now knew the answer to whether or not she wanted Joe to kiss her. Not just yes, but often.

Footsteps approaching broke them apart.

"Can I help you two?" The familiar voice held amusement.

She turned and found one of her best customers wearing a big grin.

"Sam, could you help us unwind?"

Chuckling, the older man started to reach for the dog's collar, but Noelle avoided him by standing and began walking the reverse of her earlier path. In less than a minute, they were unwrapped.

Stepping away, Molly felt the loss of Joe's warmth. "I guess Noelle was ready to set us free. Thank you for trying to help, Sam. You get a free cinnamon roll tomorrow. You can have them free all week if you don't tell anyone else about this."

"I'll take tomorrow's, but I'll have to think about the rest. This may be too good of a story to keep to myself."

Molly sighed as the man vanished into the night. She'd have people joking about this in the bakery for days if Sam told the story, which would no doubt be embellished with each telling. "We better get moving or we'll miss the whole thing."

When they arrived by the tree, Noelle sniffed nose to nose with a couple of dogs, and all was well. They all stood side by side as the lights came on the tree and everyone cheered.

Of course, when everyone cheered, Noelle let out a howl, and a couple of the dogs barked to join her. Everyone around them laughed. Molly was relieved that people seemed to enjoy Noelle's unique way of communicating.

Back at her van, Molly opened the door for Joe, and Noelle jumped into the van, settling herself in the same place as before. "I'm getting the impression that she loves to go for rides."

"That's going to be fun next summer when you can take her out for all sorts of hikes. Do you go camping?" Joe asked as they pulled away from the curb.

"I'm more a day-hiking woman. I never enjoyed that whole 'sleeping on the hard ground covered by a piece of fabric with animals out in the woods' thing. But I can hike for miles as long as I have the promise of a comfy bed under a roof at the end of the day. Besides, now that I have the bakery and only one day off a week, it would be hard for me to go on a camping trip. How about you?"

"I am honestly a city boy," he said with an embarrassed smile. "I loved hiking the few times I had the chance, but I haven't had the opportunity to do much of it. For so many years, I've been either in school or working six days a week like you. Sometimes I was doing both."

Joe directed her to his apartment. "Next summer, there are a lot of places I can take you that I think you're going to love." As soon as she said the words, she wanted to take them back and bury them deeply where he could never hear them. This had been a mistake in the past. One of her many. Never talk about a future with a man. They seem to only be able to handle one day at a time.

"I'd like that."

Molly almost slammed on the brakes. She caught herself just in time, because braking quickly on an icy road would have probably sent them skidding off the road. For the first time in her life, a man had said he wanted to do something with her in the future.

$\mathcal{M}$olly crawled into bed that night. Staying up until 9:00 p.m. sounded like nothing to most people, but it was like she'd stayed up until 2:00 a.m., considering when her alarm would sound. She needed enough sleep to be alert. It was a funny thing in the bakery business that no one appreciated burned pastries.

The following morning, she tried to smile at each customer and give each her full attention. The reality of the situation was that she kept wishing she was down the street at the clinic with Joe. She didn't want anybody else to snatch her opportunity to spend time with him. Besides, painting had been part of their deal. She needed to fulfill their agreement.

She mixed up some chocolate chocolate chip cookie dough, stowed it in the walk-in refrigerator, and headed out to pick up Noelle. When they'd parked in town and

Molly let her out of the truck, Noelle tugged her in the direction of Joe's clinic. It seemed that she knew where they were going. They stepped in the door, and Molly paused.

Joe was installing a doorknob on one of the exam room doors. As she was about to comment on the skill with which he seemed to be doing it, especially for a man who claimed to not be handy, Noelle spoke.

Joe dropped his screwdriver and jumped to his feet, whirling around to see who was there. He put his hand on his chest. "Give a guy a chance next time. Tell me you're here before she can."

The dog let out a howl as though to put an emphasis on her earlier communication.

Molly walked toward him. "How's it going?"

"I look like I know what I'm doing, don't I?" Frustration poured out of every word.

She raised an eyebrow at his comment and his tone of voice. "You do."

"That couldn't be more deceptive. I watched several videos about how to install not just a doorknob but this particular model. It didn't work at all the first time. I am hopeful about the second attempt, though."

Since Molly also had zero knowledge of doorknob installation, she decided that remaining silent on the subject was probably the higher path to take. "I can leave you to that and get started on the painting just as soon as I get her settled in the back. Sound good?"

Joe had already refocused with a furrowed brow on

the doorknob in front of him. It amazed her that a man who could be so good with technology and able to perform surgery was the opposite of a do-it-yourself guy. She had done quite a few things over the years in her bakery and in the different homes she'd lived in. Her parents had taught their children to be self-sufficient and figure things out somehow. Being able to watch videos had been a game changer.

She walked over to the cans of paint. "Orange and yellow? And purple?"

He set the screwdriver to the side and faced her. "Orange for the dog, yellow for the cat, and I thought maybe we could paint purple collars on them."

She could see his vision. "It will certainly be colorful." If a bakery customer had asked her to put those colors on a cake, she would have done her best to talk them out of it. Of course, she would have made anything they wanted, but she also would have loved for it to come out looking good. "Okay, the cat and dog I can do because Aimee's already outlined them. If you want the collars, I think we'd better ask her to come back. I'm not sure I'll be able to get the right shape on them so they don't look like tourniquets or something worse."

Joe went back to work, and from the sounds coming from his direction, Molly wondered if she should offer to help. Maybe a second set of eyes on the directions would make a difference. She decided to wait until she finished painting.

When she had, she wiped her hands on a rag, pulled

her phone out of her pocket, and saw that two hours had passed since she'd started. Standing, she stretched her sore muscles.

"What do you think?" She took a few steps back so she could get a good perspective on the animals. He actually had a pretty good eye for color. The yellow and orange looked good against the blue. It was all very vibrant and happy, and she liked that. When there was no reply, she turned around and found Joe sitting on the floor with that same doorknob beside him. She'd never seen a more dejected expression on a human being. "You weren't able to figure it out?"

He shook his head. Molly walked over and put her hand on his shoulder—as she would have for any friend. "Maybe it's just a difficult doorknob to install."

He shook his head in the same way again. "It looks easy in the videos."

"Everything looks easy when an expert is doing it. I have a feeling that it would look easy if we installed a camera in your clinic and watched you at work with animals."

He put his hand on hers where it rested on his shoulder. "Thank you, Molly. I appreciate that. It's bad enough when a man feels like he's failed, but it's much worse when there are witnesses." This time he smiled up at her.

"My dad is very good at a lot of this handyman-type stuff. For that matter, Aimee's fiancé is very good at all these things too."

"It was pretty impressive when his four brothers swept in and put up my walls."

"They actually helped build a house for Mark's wife. That's how he and Madeline got together. Would you like to call one of them or my dad for help?"

"Let's call Jack and see if he's available. I've already met most of his family, so he probably knows about my skill level." She assumed that came with the smallest dent in his male pride. "I assume he isn't taking as many photos this time of the year."

"I know he's back from his trip. He's been out shooting sunrises and sunsets off the water. And we had northern lights not long ago that he photographed."

"I would love to see the northern lights. I've seen photos of them where lights dance in the sky in different colors, but never in person."

"You'll have your chance this winter."

Molly dialed Aimee and explained what they needed. By the time she'd hung up, her friend had asked her fiancé to come over to help, and demanded to see her the next morning to find out what was going on between her and Joe. Molly could only mumble one-word replies to the questions over the phone with the man in question standing beside her.

A couple of hours later, all the doorknobs had been installed. Jack had done a genius job of including Joe in the process so he understood how to do it now and felt better about his skills. They also put up some shelving in the back and swapped out a couple of light fixtures that

Joe wanted instead of the ones that were better suited to a jewelry store.

They all walked out the door together, and Jack paused as Joe locked the door. "Aimee said she'll see you right before you open in the morning."

Molly glanced over at Joe to see if he was catching the meaning of their conversation.

"She expects a full update. Those are her words."

Molly weakly smiled as Jack grinned at her and headed down the street whistling. He and her friend made a good couple. Aimee could be so serious sometimes. He supported her and helped lighten her up.

Joe asked, "About what?"

Her embarrassment level hit a new high. "Um, about Christmas things." That was true, right? It was now Christmastime, so everything was a Christmas thing.

He watched her for a second, then seemed to accept her answer. "Ready to go?"

Noelle made one of her low talking noises, thankfully not howling like a wolf and scaring someone who might be out walking.

When she dropped Joe off at his apartment, he said, "I asked Jack if he knew anyone who could help me get the equipment out of my truck and into my clinic. Some men who work on the fishing charter aren't doing much this time of year and would be happy to help for a small moving fee. Maybe when your mom comes into work tomorrow, you can run me out to your house. I know you're busy, and I hate to ask that of you, but I think it's the best way to make it work."

Molly would get to see him again in the middle of the day? That was fine with her.

When he opened the van's door, he paused and turned back toward her. She wanted to kiss him and thought he wanted to kiss her too, but a furry obstacle sat between them. He sighed, petted Noelle, and climbed out.

Their project was almost over. His clinic would be close to opening once he had his equipment situated in there. They'd completed all the construction and most of the painting. And it looked like she had a good dog with Noelle, one who knew how to behave with other people, pets, and groups. He'd helped her see that.

There wasn't much left to learn. Class time was almost done, and so was any excuse she had to be around Joe. She had to admit to herself, as she drove home from dropping him off, that she very much wanted to spend time with him. She wasn't even sure right now if she was pursuing him or not. They'd gone from strangers to acquaintances, and this afternoon had seemed to become friends. With kissing.

CHAPTER FIFTEEN

*M*olly put a cup of coffee and a cookie in front of Aimee, then got busy with her morning work. She put sugar cookies in a box for a customer who had ordered three dozen shipped to his home in the Bush, added special packing materials, and sealed and addressed it.

With that job taken care of, she decided to take a break with her friend—even though she knew Aimee had one goal, and it wasn't idle chitchat. Why put off the inevitable?

"One of our future lessons with Noelle is going to be taking her out on a boat. Do you think you'd be able to use one of your grandfather's and take the three of us out?"

Aimee slowly lowered her cup of coffee to the table. "*Future* lessons?"

"Don't read anything into that. The man is a veterinarian who has made a huge difference in my life with Noelle." Molly stood. "Would you like to test the muffin I just pulled out of the oven? It's a triple berry."

Aimee reached out and grabbed Molly's arm. "Two things. One: when you plan a future—pretty much anything in the future—with a man, you're seeing things in a long-term-relationship way. Two: of course I want to try the muffin."

Molly rolled her eyes. "There are all different kinds of relationships. Sometimes it's just friendship. That, after all, is a relationship, right?" If she didn't think about kissing Joe, she might be able to convince her friend of that, if not herself. It wouldn't be lying, because any solid relationship with a man had to be founded on friendship.

Aimee sipped her coffee. "It is."

As Molly walked away, she heard her friend mutter, "But that isn't what this is."

Molly ignored Aimee's comment. Her friend continued her thread of conversation when Molly returned with the muffin on a plate, but she thankfully dropped the dating remarks.

"I'm sure I can take out one of Grandpa's boats. When did you want to go?"

"Let's wait until after Christmas. I'd like to be able to take a full day off. I need the holiday baking to settle down and for life to go back to a winter normal. Then I can just have Mom fill in for me for a day."

"Okay, just let me know when."

"And tell your grandfather that I will be happy to reimburse him for the cost of the fuel and whatever else is associated with the boat."

Aimee smiled widely. "And you think that my stubborn grandfather will take money from you?" She laughed. "It would make my grandparents happy to help you. In fact, I wouldn't be surprised if Grandpa wanted to be at the helm when you took Noelle out for her first ride on a boat." Aimee took a bite of the muffin and sighed. "This is so good. I think you have me test the muffins, though, because you know I love every one of them."

"No. You've been honest with me. You've told me when you loved one more than another. And there was that one that didn't work. You weren't bashful about letting me know."

Aimee shuddered. "I'm still not sure why you thought peppermint and orange would go together. I mean, maybe you can combine them somehow, but that had the same nasty taste you get when you drink orange juice not long after you brush your teeth."

"Notice that the muffin you're making disparaging remarks about never made it onto the menu."

"And that is why people love coming to your bakery. It's only the good stuff." Aimee finished her treat. "I think I've had enough sugar to start my day. It's actually not the start of my day. Like you, I'm up early this time of year." As she stood, she said, "I've been thinking. Noelle might have been out on boats lots of times. You should give Mrs. Jacobsen a call to find out. Now, I have to get back to work."

"How are your projects going?"

"I'm finishing up the wedding set today for a cute couple who came into my store several months ago. They took a while to decide on the design. She bounces on her feet and he's very calm and quiet. I think they're going to love what I've created. I'll be meeting them here at Cinnamon next week."

"I'm happy to be your office headquarters for things like that."

"Thank you. I feel so free now that I don't have the brick-and-mortar store. Sometimes the dream you thought you had wasn't the one you really wanted." Aimee headed toward the door. "It's almost time for you to open the door for your customers. Maybe I can come over tonight, and we can take the dog for a walk."

Molly felt her face heat. "Um, Joe called and offered to give me another lesson tonight after his equipment is moved into his clinic."

Aimee's eyebrows shot up. "Really? What new thing are you doing this time?"

Yeah, that was the problem. Was it a new lesson or was it more than a lesson? Molly wouldn't admit to wondering that out loud, though. It came with too much baggage attached. "We're going back for another walk on the beach."

Aimee gave a slow nod and said, "He's been to the beach before with the dog. I'm sure of that because you told me about how filthy she got, and the ordeal of bathing her."

Molly straightened her shoulders and prepared to give Aimee the same reasons for this being a lesson as she'd been telling herself. "But do you really know how to do anything well if you've only done it once? I mean, if I showed you how to bake cookies once, would you be able to repeat those results or would you need a second lesson to solidify those ideas?" That sounded even better than she'd expected.

Aimee pursed her lips and nodded. "That is good logic. You certainly have a valid point." As she opened the door, she added, "But is that really what you're thinking?" She went out the door, leaving Molly wondering about that too.

Should she cancel tonight? She gave that five seconds of thought. Absolutely not. Noelle had so much fun on the beach, and if somebody wanted to help give that dog a bath, she wasn't going to argue with them. Maybe after a couple times she would be able to do it better herself.

She hurried home from work that day. Joe pulled up in his truck soon after. They loaded Noelle into the back seat and drove to the Spit.

Molly knew she had a bounce in her step. She tried very hard not to define the reason for it, but she knew in her heart that it was because she was spending time with this man again. After fighting the emotions and pushing them away time and time again, she had to admit that she had fallen for him, and not just a little bit. She had fallen hard.

She, Molly Becker, was in love with Joseph Wiseman.

The obvious question was: how had that happened? But the answer was right in front of her. He'd gone out of his way to be kind to her, to help her, and been so much more than a friend.

She'd thought the emotions she'd felt with other men were real and important. Comparing them, she knew they hadn't been. This man tugged at her heartstrings in a way she had never imagined was possible.

Sure, he had given signs that he was interested in her, but he was also interested in her dog. She could be open to pain even more intense than before. As the full measure of the idea of loving him hit her, she leaned back against the seat.

"Are you okay?" He glanced over at her as they went down the road.

Noelle chatted from the backseat as she joined in the conversation.

"I'm fine." Was she fine? "You think we're going to have to give her another bath today?" She glanced over at him, and he grinned, which warmed her heart.

"This dog does everything with her whole heart. I don't think there's any way that she can walk away from something like this clean. She's going to be filthy."

Molly laughed. "That sounds right, doesn't it?"

When they arrived at the beach, Joe's hands were clammy from nervousness. Was this *the* night when their relationship became more serious? He'd asked to bring her back to what seemed to be one of her favorite places. Molly's and Noelle's. If the sunset over Kachemak Bay did not warm Molly's heart toward him, he would have to conclude that this would only ever be friendship and not force himself any further into her life. She'd kissed him before, but today—*if* he had the chance—he hoped to kiss her and that it would touch her heart.

When they walked out on the beach, Molly's smile grew wider with each step. They didn't find any other dogs on the beach again—winter really was a beautiful thing in a small town that relied heavily on tourists and warmer weather—so Molly unleashed the dog. Noelle raced around, exploring. Molly shivered and pulled her coat more tightly against her neck.

"Cold?" He put his arm around her and held her to his side. She seemed to become one with him, melding to him. When Noelle was a bit too far away from them, he said, "Let's walk down the beach and follow her." He took his arm from around her, and she sighed. Maybe she'd liked it as much as he did. His heart did a little happy dance. He slid his hand in hers, and their gloved hands clasped together.

Noelle raced back toward them, and Molly bubbled with laughter. She knelt and clapped her hands together. "Come here."

"She'll knock you down."

Seconds later, Molly was sprawled on her back on the beach, laughing. The dog raced away, and Joe helped

Molly to her feet. When he did, they were facing each other. He brushed strands of blonde hair off her cheek and leaned in slowly, waiting for her to stop him if this wasn't what she wanted. Instead of stopping, she put her hands on his collar and tugged him toward her. All doubts were gone as he kissed her with everything he'd been holding inside.

She wrapped her arms around him and up to his shoulders, pulling him closer, and he angled his head for a deeper kiss. When they pulled apart, he wasn't sure if it was seconds or minutes later. Hints of pink in the sky set a romantic scene.

He leaned in and kissed Molly again, and this time she was just as passionate about it as before. He had to force himself to take a step back, to give them a moment to get back to where they should be.

Noelle sat beside them as a wash of pink lit the whole sky and reflected off the water. He turned Molly around to face the sunset and wrapped his arms around her waist in front of him.

"Beautiful." She sighed.

"Yes, it is."

Did they both mean the kiss or the sunset? Either way, he hoped Molly had fallen for him every bit as much as he'd fallen for her.

Winter sunsets could be so beautiful in Homer. The white mountains and the bay were lit with color. Her heart still raced from what they'd shared, and a grin nearly split her face in two. That was the best, most wonderful kiss she had ever experienced in her life. She could happily spend the rest of her days kissing this man and this man alone.

She asked, "What are your plans for Christmas Day and Christmas Eve?"

Molly wouldn't have asked that question this morning, but now she wanted to share the holidays and every moment with him.

"I had hoped that at least my parents would be here, but I don't think either they or any of my sisters are going to make it this year. I'll survive. I spent many holidays alone or with friends in the years since I went to veterinary school. Life became too busy to go home then."

When he rested his chin on her shoulder, peace and exhilaration filled her, but how could both emotions be there?

"I graduated and found a position in a clinic halfway across the country from my parents. I will say, though, that they seemed to enjoy visiting Phoenix in December. Minnesota's a bit chillier then." He chuckled, and she felt the vibration of it against her back.

"Just a bit. I didn't realize you'd been in the desert before this. It would be warm there right now. Why Alaska?"

"I always dreamed of having a practice in a small town. Homer seemed perfect. And it does get below freezing in

Phoenix. There was a decorative waterfall at the entrance to my apartment complex. That froze one year, and snow dusted the cactus."

"That's such a bizarre concept to somebody who's from the north."

"I know. Christmas lights strung on a giant saguaro cactus is an odd sight." He shrugged.

"So you're alone this Christmas?"

"I am. Or"—he turned toward her—"at least I was."

A sigh escaped Molly before she could stop it. She sounded like a swooning girl from a historical romance novel. "I'm sure you'd be welcome to join my family. It's just my mom and my stepdad, whom I really think of as my father, right now. My brother should be flying into Homer right after Christmas."

"I'd like that. Can I take you out to dinner tomorrow?"

The two of them alone? That sounded like a date. "Yes. I would like that."

He suggested a restaurant that was a short walk from her bakery.

"I'll run home to let Noelle out when Mom comes in. She'll be fine then until after dinner."

Her heart felt full. A date. And her family and Joe together for the holidays. Everything was going *very* well.

CHAPTER SIXTEEN

For the next few days, Molly floated on a cloud of bliss. She baked dozens of Christmas sweets, took care of Noelle, and spent time with Joe. The date had gone well and ended with another spectacular kiss. Well, more than one of those kisses.

Her world felt right and wonderful. She had another dinner date planned with Joe tonight.

After taking two pans of pinwheel cookies out of the oven, she took her turn working with customers in the front of her café.

A large man entered the bakery and glanced around, almost like he was searching for someone. He looked like he should be a linebacker on a football team or at least like he could have been one a couple of decades earlier.

She went over to him. "I'm Molly. Can I help you?"

"Molly? You're exactly the person I'm looking for." He

wrapped his arms around her in a bear hug, squeezed her tightly, and stepped back, grinning.

Molly searched for a way to call for help if needed without causing too big of a disturbance in her almost-full restaurant.

"I'm Reuben Wiseman. Joe's dad."

Her nervousness subsided. "It's a pleasure to meet you, sir."

He waved his hand and said, "Dispense with that 'sir' stuff. You're all my son has spoken about since my wife and I arrived yesterday and surprised him." Then he frowned. "You've been a big distraction for my boy as he's prepared for this next phase of his life."

Molly's heart started beating fast again. A distraction? That didn't sound like a good thing, did it?

Before she could reply, he continued, "Yes. He had definite plans for the future, and you have ripped those apart, shredded them, and stomped them into the ground." He smiled, but she wasn't sure if it was a friendly smile after his words.

In a voice she barely recognized, Molly said, "I'm sorry if I disrupted his way of life."

The man roared with laughter. "Disrupted? See here, there isn't anything left of what I expected to find when I got here. All except for his clinic, which looks great. I understand that your artistry is responsible for some of that."

"It's really my friend Aimee's artistry."

"It's very professional. Now, I'd like to take some of

those sweet baked goods you've been tempting my son with back to our hotel room."

Molly forced a smile, her challenging-customer smile that she'd perfected over the last couple of years. "Of course, sir. I mean Reuben."

The man left with a box of cinnamon rolls and a couple of her favorite holiday muffin flavors.

One of Molly's regular customers came over and patted her shoulder. "Molly, I'm sorry."

She turned to him. "What?"

"That sounded like a man who didn't want you in his son's life, didn't it?"

Molly's eyes dropped toward the floor. She felt like she couldn't look anyone in the eye right now. An entire restaurant of people had heard the man's words. Had he meant that? She wasn't sure. "I never intended to take Joe away from his work."

"I'm sure you didn't." He adjusted his suspenders slightly and said, "I know what will distract you from your sorrow."

Now Molly looked him in the eye. "What? Closing?"

"Getting me one of those cinnamon rolls and warming it up a bit."

She tried to smile, and this time failed. No matter what, though, she had her business and her customers.

She'd be okay. She had thought this Christmas would be different. That Joe would be part of it as her special someone. She wasn't sure what to make of his father's words, but no matter what, he had his family here, so he didn't need to be with her and her family.

Molly pulled out everything she needed and got to work on a massive batch of bread. She *could* knead it with the mixer—but not this batch. She would turn coal into silver by making a limited-edition Christmas bread. She had discovered long ago that if she wanted to take out frustrations on anything, kneading bread was the way to go.

"Honey, are you okay?" her mom asked from beside her as she added ingredients. Her mother's work shift hadn't started when Joe's dad had been there, so she'd missed the show.

"I have an idea for some bread for the season." Molly focused on the task, and away from what had happened.

"I'm sure that will be well received. What are you going to put in it?"

Molly kept working as she thought about the answer. All she knew for sure was that she wanted to beat some bread dough into oblivion. "Spices, maybe some currants and dried apples."

"That sounds delicious. An apple spice bread."

Molly continued working as her idea came to life. "Maybe with frosting across it like you do with hot cross buns."

"Yum. If you want to work on that, I'll take care of customers the rest of the afternoon."

"Thanks, Mom." That fit in well with her plans because she was afraid she would burst into tears if anyone tried to have a conversation with her beyond baking. When she finished making the dough, she left it to rise and took care of other tasks like restocking the cases and starting another pot of coffee.

As she worked, Molly could hear Reuben's words replaying in her mind. They didn't make sense to her. And why had he hugged her if he planned to accuse her of ruining his son's life? She and Joe hadn't talked about their feelings, but she'd thought that he cared about her, maybe more than just cared.

When everyone had left and she'd closed the bakery, she divided the dough that had now risen nicely into single-loaf portions. She kneaded it, threw on some flour, and kneaded it some more, the flour poofing into the air. Loaf by loaf, she waited for her stress level to drop as it usually did, but not this time.

So what if Joe considered her to be a distraction? Sure, she'd fallen for him, but she'd get over it. Broken hearts mended.

She tried to rein in her emotions, but she felt out of control. Taking a deep breath, she focused on the bread and nothing else, as she took out another portion of the dough and continued working.

She wasn't sure how much time had passed since she'd closed, but she knew it must have been hours. When someone knocked on the door, she yelped, and the dough she'd been working with dropped from her hands to the bakery table. Their face at the door was obscured because she was in light and it was already dark out. She pointed at the sign on the door and shouted "Closed!"

That person pounded louder and louder. She finally threw the dough onto the counter, spraying even more flour into the air, and stomped over to the door. Who couldn't read the sign? She saw Joe's face peering around it and stopped. She really did not want to have this conversation right now. His dad had said everything that needed to be said, hadn't he? He pleaded with his eyes and she could read his mouth as he said, "Please."

She unlocked the door with a sigh and pulled it open, but she did not step back so that he could enter. "Why are you here?"

An expression of hurt and confusion popped onto his face. "You were supposed to meet me for dinner. I was worried. What's wrong?"

When a couple walked down the sidewalk laughing, she stepped backward and motioned Joe inside, locking the door behind him so no one else could come in. "Joe, your dad came in this morning."

His face lit up. "He's a big, blustering guy, but a teddy bear at heart. At least that's what everyone says. He's the family medicine doctor everyone wants to have. Friendly and smiling, but telling it like it is." He tilted his head to the side and looked at her. "It sounds like he told you something that upset you. What?"

So they *were* having this discussion now. It felt too raw and on the surface for her to contain herself too much longer. "Joe, he told me I had been a distraction in your life. That you had focused for many years to get where you were, and now I was pulling you away from that."

She stared down at her hands and added in a low voice, "I don't want to be a hindrance to anyone's life. I didn't meet you for dinner tonight because we're done. I was so worried about how falling for you would make it harder for me to focus on my business that I never stopped to think that maybe I was keeping you from yours. I should have, though, shouldn't I?"

"That's it?"

"What do you mean? I'm hurting your life. I understand, I'm sorry, and I am walking away."

He pulled her into a hug, and she pushed against his chest. "Molly, you're the best thing that has ever happened to me. Are you distracting me? Yes! Thank you! My entire life has been filled with school and classes and more training. It's gone on and on for years. My parents constantly tell me every time they see me that they want me to have a life, to expand myself beyond work. You did that." He put his hands on her cheeks and leaned forward to kiss her.

Molly blinked rapidly to hold back tears. "Do you mean that I shouldn't leave your life?"

He wrapped his arms around her and pulled her close. "Molly, you scared me so much. I don't know what would happen to me if you left right now. You're important to me."

Important. Was that like love?

"I love you, Joseph Wiseman." As soon as she'd said the

words, she winced. *Way to go, Molly, exposing your emotions even more.*

When he laughed, she pushed against him so she could get away.

"Please don't misunderstand me. I love you too. It seems like I have forever, but you are so skittish that it felt foolish for me to fall for you so quickly."

At that, floodgates opened. Tears streamed down her face.

He reached up and wiped her cheek. "Doesn't flour and salty water make glue?"

She nodded. "I think it does. But I don't care." She laughed through the tears. "You're covered in flour."

"That's because you are. I've never seen you like that, so you must've been taking out some aggressions on an unsuspecting batch of baked goods. Am I right?"

"So right!"

"I told my parents I was coming to check on you."

"I should probably finish up the bread I'm making. I'd hate for it to go to waste."

"That would be unfortunate. Can I help?"

She linked her arm in his as they walked to her work area. "Are you any better at baking than you are with painting and do-it-yourself projects?"

His throaty laugh made her smile. "Probably not. But I'm a good helper."

"I don't want to be alone."

"Me, either."

She leaned forward and kissed him, gently at first and

then wrapping her arms around his neck and pulling him tighter against her. They stayed like that until someone walked by and catcalled.

She jumped back from him with her hand over her mouth. "That was so embarrassing."

"Yeah, it was. I'm not usually a public-display-of-affection kind of guy. But there's something about you."

"Wash your hands, Joe. Let's make bread to redirect your thoughts."

Grinning, he did as she'd asked.

*M*olly had looked forward to Valentine's Day for weeks. She'd never had a boyfriend on that day in the past. It seemed like everyone else got the flowers, candy, special dinners out, and sweet nothings whispered in their ears. She never had. She had a feeling that Joe might be the guy to change that.

He arrived not long after she got home from work. Noelle hurried over to him and chattered away, greeting him as he entered the house. He rubbed her head and behind her ears, her favorite thing in the world—well, after running outside and treats.

He held up a package. "I got her a doggy backpack. That way when we go on hikes, she can carry her own water and food. I'm going to put it on her today. I thought we could let her run around outside with it every once in a while to get used to it before it's warm enough to actually use the backpack on a hike."

She shrugged her agreement. She wasn't one of those people who were greedy for gifts, but she was disappointed that Noelle got a Valentine's gift and she did not. Maybe he had a backpack for her too. She chuckled to herself.

She picked up the book she'd been reading. Nothing could make her forget the moment more than a good story. Not too much later, she heard the door open and Joe said, "Noelle and I want to show you something. Call her over."

Glancing up from her book, she saw Noelle standing there with the cutest backpack on. It was purple and had pockets on both sides. Right now it looked like fresh flowers were stuffed into one of the pockets.

Molly called her dog over. "Come on. Let me see what you have there." As she did that, she realized that Joe had vanished. He must have had to do something else outside.

Noelle happily trotted over. Molly rubbed her ears first as a greeting, which earned her some chatter. Then she pulled out what turned out to be a dozen roses. They were a stunning mixture of colors: red, yellow, orange, pink, and white.

Then she realized something was sticking out of the pouch on the other side, so she reached in for it. This time, she found a box of candy, but not chocolate. This was a dog-friendly assortment that didn't have dog toxins like chocolate. Heart-shaped gummies and all sorts of cute candies for the holiday lay inside the box.

When Noelle turned, Molly noticed a ribbon around

her neck, and dangling from it was a small bag. Molly untied the bow and lifted it away. When she tipped the bag upside down, a small jewelry box fell out, one she recognized as being from Aimee's business. She opened it and found the most beautiful engagement and wedding ring set she had ever seen nestled inside the velvet.

She'd know this design style anywhere. Aimee had made these. A row of diamonds across the top of the engagement ring had fine swirls of yellow gold around the white gold settings. Molly had always commented on the rings that Aimee made that had a delicate, feminine touch, and those with mixed metals. She'd also said that if she forgot to take her jewelry off before she got into some dough, she might never get it out of some types of settings. Aimee had taken everything she had said and combined it with some of Joe's knowledge about her too, because these rings had a unique style all their own.

She heard footsteps and looked up. Joe must have darted down the hallway when he let the dog in the door and watched her open her gifts. He licked his lips nervously as he knelt in front of her. Taking her hand in his, he gazed into her eyes. "Molly, it has been my honor to get to know you the last few months. Would you do me the honor of being my wife?"

Noelle chattered as Joe spoke.

"Of course, I'll marry you!" She leaned forward and they kissed.

Noelle chattered some more.

"I think she wants us to know that you're marrying both of us."

He laughed. "That's true. I accept that agreement, Noelle." She nuzzled him with her muzzle. "I had hoped you would say yes, Molly. I also hope you don't mind that I contacted Mrs. Jacobsen with a question."

What on earth could he have asked Mrs. Jacobsen about?

"I don't mind, but I don't understand."

"I know you said you couldn't afford to buy this house. That it was much more house—I believe your words were 'twice as much house' as you thought you could afford for your first home."

"Exactly."

"The two of us together can buy it, and Mrs. Jacobsen has agreed to make the asking price very affordable. She's so happy you took Noelle and are caring for her in such a loving way. She wants Noelle to have this home to run and play in. Besides," he added with a shrug, "she thought it was great that there was going to be an on-site, twenty-four-seven veterinarian."

Molly laughed. "This is the best Valentine's Day ever. I was so worried before that a matchmaker would stick his or her nose in my business, but we fell in love without one."

"*Our* business." He kissed her.

~

Noelle watched her humans. It hadn't been easy to get these two together, but she was proud of her work. Every step of the way, Molly and Joe had fought against falling in love. She'd done everything she could to help.

Joe had tried to kiss Molly before she was ready, but she'd stopped that by howling. She'd known when it was time, though. To this moment, she thought her crowning accomplishment was spinning around them with her leash.

Never let it be said that a dog didn't know about romance. Besides, having a veterinarian as a pet parent might be helpful. He might also bring home a handsome malamute for her.

They all stared at the sparkling thing on Molly's finger. When Joe kissed Molly again, Noelle talked to tell them she approved.

WHAT'S NEXT?

Thank you for reading Joe, Molly, and Noelle's story!

If you enjoyed this fun, sweet book, check out Accidentally Matched, the first book in the Alaska Matchmakers romance series. Noah and Rachel think they'll only spend a short time together, but nothing goes as planned. They're soon stuck together on an Alaska adventure. Add in matchmakers (not just one) to make it a story you won't want to miss.

There's a FREE, short story tied to the Alaska romances. Pete and Cathy are in *Falling for Alaska*. Pete—Nathaniel's lawyer—and Cathy—a woman on a hike with Jemma—are minor characters, but their cute first meeting is a FREE short story. I liked them so much that I brought them back in book three, *Crazy About Alaska*. Get it at cathrynbrown.com/together.

ABOUT THE AUTHOR

Writing books that are fun and touch your heart

Even though Cathryn Brown always loved to read, she didn't plan to be a writer. Cathryn felt pulled into a writing life, testing her wings with a novel and moving on to articles. She's now an award-winning journalist who has sold hundreds articles to local, national, and regional publications.

The Feather Chase, written as Shannon L. Brown, was her first published book and begins the Crime-Solving Cousins Mystery series. The eight-to-twelve-year-olds in your life will enjoy this contemporary twist on a Nancy Drew–type mystery.

Cathryn's from Alaska and has two series of clean Alaska romances. You can start reading with *Falling for Alaska*, or with *Accidentally Matched* in the spin-off series.

Cathryn enjoys hiking, sometimes while dictating a book. She also unwinds by baking and reading. Cathryn lives in Tennessee with her professor husband and adorable calico cat.